I083B643

Free Gift

Thank you for your purchase. To claim your free gift please visit www.CTPFiction.com

COLLECTIVE FANTASY

AN UNSAVORY ANTHOLOGY

A Collective Tales Publishing Anthology

Collective Fantasy
An Unsavory Anthology

Cover design © 2021 by Collective Tales Publishing
Cover designed by Natasha MacKenzie
Edited by Elizabeth Suggs, Jonathan Reddoch, Alex Child, Brandon Prows, and Zoë Freeman

Contents

Introduction

Following the success of our horror anthologies *Collective Darkness*, *Little Darkness*, and *The Darkness Between*, we wanted to delve deeper into the fantasy element. But we didn't want cutesy run-of-the-mill fairytales. We wanted something darker. Something deadlier. So, we crawled into seedy, crime-infested kingdoms to deliver to you *Collective Fantasy: An Unsavory Anthology*.

We start with "Poached Caladrius Eggs" by Alex Child, one of our returning authors. We follow an elf, a dwarf, and a fawn who poach a rare magical egg in the heart of a dead city.

Our tales take you to dark alleys, underground jousting tournaments, dungeons, crumbling castles, rotting battlefields, and abandoned towns. The cast of characters includes cunning thieves, lethal assassins, powerful witches, cult-fanatics, grotesque monsters, and even more thieves.

We close our anthology with "Games" by our youngest author (only 17 when she wrote this), Anne Gregg, a tale of a deadly assassin tasked by a princess with retrieving three ancient weapons of unspeakable power.

Collective Fantasy plays in the grimy underbelly of the mystical realm, exploring themes of murder, dishonesty, and betrayal. You'll be spellbound by these inglorious delights.

Jonathan Reddoch - Elizabeth Suggs
CTPFiction.com
Collective Tales Publishing

Poached Caldrius Eggs

Alex Child

The prison wagon rocked between two flanking marble towers lining the city gate. Its occupants included Lyria the expert poacher, Torvin the dwarven banker, and Goroth the belligerent orc. Awestruck by the magnificent yet crumbling alabaster walls, Torvin was briefly apathetic to their imprisonment and impending doom.

Shattering the silence, the orc said, "Disorderly conduct and public urination," he belched, "And you two?"

"We stole some horses," Lyria said.

Torvin sighed. *What have we gotten ourselves into?*

Lyria nudged him, "I told you; this was the only way."

Lyria clenched the pits of her arm shut tight with every bump in the road to ensure the smuggled knife contained within remained in place. The wagon halted abruptly at the center of the deserted town square. Armed guards stepped down and peered into the wagon; dark eyes studied the captives from behind clay masks. The figures were draped in fraying burlap robes. They slowly circled around, unlocking the cage door. The three prisoners spilled onto the cobblestone with relief.

"Those constables were… abnormal," Torvin said.

"They're not constables; they're Undaunted," Lyria hissed.

Knowing the Undaunted by their fearsome reputation, Torvin nodded, "I wish you'd warned me." Lyria shrugged. They were cultists of Barovich the Ravenous, sworn to guard sources of dark magic, such as the hallowed menagerie that was the abandoned city of Harenburg. The only two ways within its resilient stone walls were in shackles, or a cultist robe.

"Seems strange the king would trust guards loyal to an arcane cleric," Torvin said.

"They don't work for pay. They work for the glory of Barovich the Ravenous and his priests," Lyria said.

The orc chimed in, "If their fragile masks are ever shattered, another Undaunted is obligated to execute them."

Lyria grunted, "The Undaunted are emptied husks, only good at one thing: splitting people open, and they're damn good at it."

Torvin rubbed his hands together, hoping those were just rumors.

"Wait," Lyria said with outstretched arms. "Quiet!"

The group paused and Lyria gestured to a small alleyway, then to her pointed ears. All was silent to her companions, then they heard a scratching like fingernails run over stone.

Lyria drew a small blade concealed within the pit of her arm and whispered to the orc, "Good luck."

She grabbed Torvin by the collar, dragging him across the town square and inside a vacant doorway. She fought shattered wooden beams for a place to hide. With lowered heads, Lyria and Torvin peered across the square.

Goroth stretched, twisting his arms behind his back as four scarlet-skinned implings darted from the shadows. Bellowing with the strength of a warhorn, the massive orc charged the growing swarm.

"What in perdition are those!" Torvin asked.

"Implings. Small, weak, but very aggressive in large numbers," replied Lyria.

Goroth crushed an implings head beneath his heel and cackled. The cracking of bone and bloodied teeth played like a macabre orchestra. It wasn't long before the bloody symphony reached a crescendo, and no more was heard from the orc.

"Understand now why my fee is so high?" Lyria said to Torvin. "The city may house a graceful caladrius whose eggs are capable of healing your daughter. But most creatures here are not so benign."

Torvin twirled the loose strands of fiber in his prison rags around his fingertips and sighed.

"This would have been far easier on my own," Lyria said.

"Would you really expect me to trust a thief? Even if you returned with exotic eggs, how would I know they were authentic?" replied Torvin.

"We need to keep moving. We can camp after we've secured shelter." She tugged on Torvin's thin clothing, leaving a tear. "The caladrius leave their nest in the morning, just after it's eaten and settled into its nest. We need to take the eggs before then."

Faint light from an overhead barrier spread across the city revealed crumbling arches and elaborate doorways festering with vegetation and mold. Muffled squawking like a group of strangled magpie resounded through the air, then everything fell silent. Lyria stepped in front of Torvin, pressing him against the wall with her back. She held up the flimsy two inch knife she'd smuggled in, silently wishing she had a dagger.

"What is it?" Torvin asked, "The implings?"

She ignored him, her knuckles tightening over the paltry weapon; mind racing. Thinking through a list of nocturnal predators, she realized with dread she had likely never encountered half of the creatures inhabiting the city. Something howled from a distance, and the dim outline of a stocky humanoid came into focus. Torvin began shaking.

"Shush; it's alright," Lyria said. She steadied her right hand behind her head, ready to fling her blade.

From the shadows emerged a hooded figure draped in dark robes with hands raised to the sides of its cowl. Lyria fired the knife from her hand. It whistled with the strength and accuracy of a crossbow bolt, embedding itself within the creature's chest up to the hilt. Blood rained from the coarse incision, and the being chuckled.

"What impeccable aim," it said.

Even in the sun's absence, Lyria made out the rough features of a heavily scarred fawn within the dark cloak. She picked up a rock and cocked back her arm.

"I assure you that of all the creatures confined within these walls, I am the least deserving of your aggression," said the fawn, smiling as he yanked the weapon from his chest. He wiped it clean, and tossed it back to Lyria who caught it without breaking eye contact, still holding the rock.

Torvin attempted to expunge himself from behind Lyria, but she snapped him back into place whispering, "Stay put, damn you."

"My name is Alton. And while I understand your suspicion, I urge you to relax. It's too late for your fellow inmate, but I can still help you. I pity all who are left to such a barbaric doom and offer my assistance."

Alton bowed; shadows sunk within pockmarks covering the fawn's face, which was otherwise round and boyish. Lyria's arm tensed.

"I think he can be of use to us," Torvin said from beneath Lyria's protective stance.

Without warning, Alton's arm darted, sending a throwing knife sailing through the air. Lyria shoved Torvin to the ground. The projectile passed just over the pair's shoulder, striking an enormous green eye surrounded by contorting tree limbs and whipping vines. The arboreous titan reared back thrashing wildly in blind torment.

"Run! Now!" cried Alton.

The trio ran beneath a nearly-collapsed archway, stumbling over piles of rubble and stone littering the street. The group ran an entire block down an isolated boulevard.

"This way," said Alton, directing them into an alleyway. He raised an illuminated gem over the wall, which waivered lightly as if it were melting, then stepped through.

Lyria halted before following, her lingering distrust stil festering. Approaching from the street, crawled the vengeful titan, ichor spraying from its wounded eye as it shrieked after them.

Panting, Lyria and Torvin tumbled through the facade. Lyria's eyes adapted almost immediately to the dim, shambled room. Wooden crates lined the walls as makeshift tables, covered with books, tools, and candle stubs.

"Welcome, friends, to my home," said Alton. A guttural screech echoed from the narrow alley they'd escaped from. Outside, a large winged creature could be heard swooping fiercely from above.

Noticing the grayed pallor of Torvin's face, Alton said, "No reason to worry, friend. In addition to providing ocular hindrance, my clypeus barrier prevents the entry of unwelcome guests."

Lyria scanned the assorted surgical tools and glass vials scattered across the room. "I believe it is time to begin more formal introductions." Their host bowed, revealing his silver tipped horns. "I'm Alton Sumerton, former premier of the now extinct White Whispers Clan."

"I'm Lyria; this is Torvin. We were arrest—"

Torvin interrupted, "I am the head manager of acquisitional expenditure at Dawes Financial Servicing. I hired her to help me collect a caladrius egg. I wish to use its medicinal properties to cure my dying daughter of porcelain fever."

Alton smiled, "It seems you have a keen sense for hired talent, Torvin."

"They say the only famous criminals are in dungeons. Lyria is the exception," Torvin said. "And I'd be a fool to leave her, or anyone really, alone with eggs worth more than the entire royal fleet."

Lyria smirked and Alton chuckled.

"Well, friends, in Harenburg guests are always welcome," Alton said. "Relax, enjoy the spoils of my cupboard, whatever you like. I treat my obligations as a host seriously."

"High time we ate; I'm starving!" Torvin proclaimed with much gusto.

Torvin raced for the open cupboard brimming with salted meat and wheels of cheese.

Lyria and Alton ignored the dwarf's boisterous chewing, instead poring over maps and tables to discuss the city's layout and its various creatures. Their host seemed hospitable enough, yet she noticed his scattered tomes were covered with arcane symbols, symbols you would never see on any respectable mage's bookshelf.

As they readied for bed a short time later Alton said, "Tomorrow I will help you find your caladrius egg. It dwells in high places, and the highest branch in the city is upon the great syracuse tree at the town's center." With a snap of his fingers he extinguished the room's candles and said, "We will venture there come sunrise."

* * *

Alton played three staccato notes from his worn nautilus-shell flute, calling three bipedal creatures matted with fur.

"Crags?" asked Lyria, staring at the oversized hairy beetles.

"Western hardshell crags," corrected Alton.

"They smell worse than the back alley of a butcher shop," complained Torvin.

"They are pungent, but they're incredibly hardy and doubtlessly subservient," Alton said as his companions reluctantly mounted their steeds.

En route to the great sycarus tree, Alton regaled them with tales of his run-ins with the city's beasts as if he were reciting from a children's book.

The raw conviction in his voice and the gleeful display of his many scars brought plausibility to each incredible encounter. One of which ran jaggedly down the length of his left arm in the color of undercooked steak.

"That damned wyvern tried to pluck me off the ground. Only took my cloak though, the fool," Alton said.

Lyria had long since stopped listening and was tossing her small blade to herself.

"You must have some stories of your own if mine bore you," Alton said, "I don't believe that's one of my knives. It looks too small to be useful here."

Lyria replied, "This dagger was enchanted by a priestess of Dovara. Hopefully, you won't see it's worth." For it's enchanted to never miss its target, she thought to herself. Alton laughed, and promptly explained how he'd escaped a harpy's nest using only a sharp stone.

The group continued, taking turns passing over a bridge Alton warned would only support their weight, leaving their crags behind.

"It's the only bridge to this borough still standing," Alton said, shouting over the putrid moat beneath them.

Over the following few hours, Lyria successfully tuned out the drone of Torvin's increasingly heavy breathing and Alton's stories. She was grateful when they arrived at a magnificent orange tree that had reclaimed an entire city block.

Alton declared, "Now for the work of retrieving the eggs. I'm happy to volunteer, though there may be a better candidate."

"I paid for the eggs. My servant shall retrieve them. The going price for such eggs could easily pay for any injuries incurred during their collection," Torvin said.

Lyria was halfway up the tree before Torvin finished extrapolating on the intricacies of egg-based economics. She expertly sprung from one branch to the next with gymnastic finesse. Alton cheered by stamping his hooves and clapping excitedly from below as she approached the nest.

Standing on a branch thick as a broom handle, she delicately tiptoed with both arms extended for balance. With the nest in reach, her arms pivoted gently forward, grasping bits of straw and twigs. Frustrated, she inched forward impatiently.

Her fingers wrapped around an egg, but she lost her footing. A single cabbage-sized egg rolled out of her reach and splattered below.

Frantically clutching the remaining two eggs to her chest, she reversed until her back collided with an outstretched tree limb. Her body twisted, and she fell like a bundle of straw until her lower leg cracked around a large branch. Innate reflex sent her arms flailing, wrapping around the tree's center, releasing the eggs. Alton's arms shot up like bowstrings before the eggs fell more than a few feet. He muttered calmly, his rhythmic chanting juxtaposed to Lyria's pained grunting. Even in her momentary paralysis, Lyria was impressed to see the two large eggs gently descend to the ground. Alton's voice fell silent, and Torvin greedily grabbed the two precious treasures.

With meticulous effort, she clambered down the enormous tree, suppressing cries of pain with each drop. Eventually, she stumbled from the ground and crumpled, groaning. Alton handed the two eggs to Torvin and approached Lyria.

"Your leg is broken in at least three places," Alton said. "Can you stand?"

Lyria hopped on one leg, bracing her weight against the tree. Ignoring Alton's extended arms, she hopped a few feet, and collapsed once more.

"Just carry her; we can put her back on the crag soon," Torvin said.

"I need my hands free to protect us," replied Alton. "And traveling with a cripple could keep us out until nightfall. She needs treatment. She needs..."

Torvin looked at his prizes. "No, she can make it. She's strong enough. I have my daughter's bark-skin to consider!"

Alton's tone fell. "Give her an egg, Torvin. You'll still have what you need for your daughter."

With a whimper, Torvin handed the smaller egg to Alton.

"The surest cure would be to poach the egg, but considering our circumstances, you'll need to eat it raw," Alton said. He cracked a hole in the shell and tilted Lyria's head back.

"Open wide," he said.

Skin stretched taut over her face in agony, Lyria obeyed. A thick yellow slurry oozed down the back of her throat. The surprisingly spicy egg lit her throat aflame. She suppressed an itching cough with a bowed head.

An excruciating fifteen minutes passed with the bulging shards of broken bone visibly regressing into position beneath her skin. No longer in pain, Lyria jumped to her feet.

"Of all the broken bones I've had mended, that was by far the fastest. And the most painful," she said.

"Exactly why the caladrius is rumored to be extinct and fools are willing to risk their lives to even get just one of their eggs," Alton said with a smirk.

On their return journey, Alton again shared stories as afternoon became evening. Upon their arrival at Alton's lair, Alton sighed as Torvin rushed once more to the pantry. Lyria barely noticed the movement in the dim candle light.

"Torvin, as a banker, I assume you can also tell a good investment from a bad one?" Alton asked.

Torvin nodded, tearing a huge bite off an oversized sausage.

"Lyria, I can feel your strength in the air around you. Your current abilities would provide me with a wonderful foundation upon which we could make you a more capable thief and poacher than you ever dreamed."

"I like to think I'm plenty capable already," Lyria said.

Alton said, "One could always improve. It's clear that even for an elf, your keen senses and physical abilities exceed most trained acrobats. I can make you something more. Something... otherworldly."

Alton cleared his throat and continued, "There is a price. An investment, you might say. Torvin, my stout friend, come here."

"What could you want with him?" Lyria asked. She looked back at the pile of books. One was opened to a page containing the symbols for sacrificial endowment and life-force consumption.

Alton glanced at her and said, "I want to make an investment out of our dear dwarven banker."

Lyria's arm snapped in position over her shoulder, ready to throw her blessed knife as she stammered, "Don't move, Torvin."

The dumbfounded dwarf, only now aware their conversation concerned him in some way, turned from the cupboard with a chunk of pickled herring suspended in his beard.

Alton sneered, "I could make you a goddess."

Her arms shaking, Lyria managed to whisper, "No. I'm obligated to prevent any harm from coming to him."

Alton snapped, "As if you could stop me."

An ethereal spark ignited, and Alton was immaterial, a blue transparent shadow. His form hovered across the ramshackle tables, leaving a wake of disturbed objects.

"Let me teach you," Alton's voice echoed.

Torvin stood mouth agape, staring at Lyria.

"All I have to do is drain him," said the ghastly voice.

Sweat loosened her grip as her fingers wrapped around the familiar hilt of her holy blade. In the split second available to her, her mind gauged Alton's speed and his remaining distance to Torvin. A thousand sinews snapped across her body like a ballista, firing.

The weapon soared, hissing just past Alton's nose. He rematerialized without noticing the blade pause midair, a mere inch from the wall. Torvin's body shook violently beneath Alton's gaze. Dovara's blessing redirected the knife, sending it straight into the back of Alton's skull. With bugged eyes, the fawn collapsed into Torvin, dislodging the chunk of fish stuck in his beard.

Fighting off her trembling, Lyria said, "Torvin, grab anything that looks useful and let's go. The sun has nearly set."

Torvin swallowed a mouthful of goat cheese before tearing through a set of cabinets. They scoured the room's contents, tossing glass vials, medical tools, and clothing into an expanding pile. It was near the back of the closet that Lyria found them.

"Are those…" Alton asked.

"Undaunted garb, yes. Put this on," Lyria snapped.

Torvin obeyed. The ragged fabric made their skin

prickle in discomfort, and the masks only offered a pinprick view. With darkness approaching, Torvin held the egg and Lyria guided them down one dark street after another toward the city gate. They had nearly arrived when a pair of footsteps echoed from a nearby alleyway.

"We're close enough, those are probably Undaunted. Slow down, act casual, and we'll be fine," Lyria whispered.

Lyria inhaled deeply, cursing at the mask's paltry slit she had to breathe through. A dim glow of torchlight spilled onto the main boulevard as the others drew closer, and something sliced open her back. It dug ferociously and carved across her spine before she fell onto the pavement. Grasping behind her, she felt Torvin bury the blade into her back and pull the blessed knife from her hip.

"The first half of your fee was high enough," Torvin whispered, "There is no sick daughter, and you were a fool to believe a word I said."

She gasped desperately for breath despite her overfilled lungs and reached fruitlessly for the dagger in her back, thin wisps of skin flapped against the sealed wound.

Torvin crept beneath the shadow of an archway to avoid the approaching guards, cradling the remaining egg.

Lyria's mind ran like a fearful horse while her body twisted in protest to the gushing wound on her back. She knew that within a few minutes she would likely pass out. The spur of limited time brought her scattered thoughts into focus.

She drew in a deep, painful breath through the small mouth opening, commanding the muscles in her arms to prop herself up. Crying out in pain, she felt her muscles tense around the blade in her back.

The two Undaunted finally appeared from the alleyway, and Lyria reached for the large rock just in front of her. Lyria resigned herself to accept whatever fate Dovara would give her, and a sudden calm instilled in her body. With specks of blood spouting from her lips, she muttered a silent prayer, asking only for another moment of control over her body.

Dovara must have been listening. Lyria grabbed the stone with whitened knuckles, and before Torvin had time to react, struck him in the face with it. The collision spread plaster shards across the road, sending Torvin to the ground. He dropped the caladrius egg which splattered on the pavement. No longer in the shadows, he was easily noticed by the two Undaunted guards.

His face now illuminated by torchlight, she could see Torvin glaring at her from beneath wet dollops of blood. Lyria turned and saw the two Undaunted draw their swords. One of them, shouting at Torvin said, "The defiled shards of your false face show you have violated your covenant to Barovich the Ravenous. You are hereby sentenced to a shameful death." Trembling, Torvin pulled himself to his feet and bolted.

The dwarf ran for all he was worth, but his short legs could only pump so fast. It wasn't long before Torvin was pinned to the ground, limbs flailing.

Lyria, surprised at how energizing it felt to see her enemy near his death, clawed her hands into the cobblestone. Her fingernails cracked and bled as she crawled toward the pooled yolk, as the Undaunted shouted scripture over Torvin's pleas for mercy.

Too frantic to notice the dull thud of Torvin's beheading, Lyria peeled up her mask, and slurped the puddled egg with a shaking tongue. The spice burned her throat once more but she didn't cough. Her vision blurred and her body began feeling as if it were empty and detached, like a floating lantern.

The world spun around her and it felt as if she were dreaming when one of the Undaunted leaned down to her and said, "May Barovich continue culling the weak from among us. If you would die then do so quickly and quietly in glory."

With those encouraging words, the two guards turned and walked down the street, one cleaning their bloodied sword against their forearm. She became conscious of the cold stone beneath her hands. Her lips quivering, a phrase took shape in her barely cognizant mind and danced on her lips.

Dying...

Dying tonight...

Her eyes fluttered and the spinning world slowed as her breath stabilized. One of the Undaunted turned from down the road and stared at her. He said something she couldn't yet understand.

Not dying tonight...

I'm not dying tonight...

A warmth spread from her belly, and her eyes shot open. The crimson river flowing from the wound in her back sealed up. She pressed both hands into the ground and slowly brought herself to her knees. The two Undaunted walked toward her.

She drew air like a bellows. Clutching the dagger in her back she gritted her teeth, and yanked. It clattered against the stone pavement as she took her first steps.

The eastern mountains were alight in hues of orange and red, a beautiful tribute to the day nearly passed, and ominous warning of the coming darkness.

I'm not dying tonight...

The thought rang through her head like a church bell. It bounced off the walls of her skull and resonated in the muscles of her leg, giving her the strength to take one. More. Step.

Then another.

And another.

Her back was still damp, but her eyesight was returning. A spark of hope ignited an inferno in her gut and now it was a joyous declaration rather than a plea, *I'm not dying tonight!*

Pulse pounding, her steps became firm and deliberate. She stood over Torvin's body and retrieved the holy blade from beside his headless corpse. As she sheathed the blade, the two Undaunted greeted her with a passing glance.

The trio exited the city for their meager camp, just as night fell. She pretended to fall asleep, then stole away under cover of darkness.

The Emerald Seed

Elizabeth Suggs

I often dreamed of an abandoned dungeon, one that I remembered as a newly orphaned youth. When I was awake, I had mourned for the loss of my parents in this place, but in my dreams, my eyes were dry. I found it almost pleasant to roam the desolate halls, exploring empty cells and discarded possessions.

In this sleep world, I played games with a girl named Cassandra. She was dressed in rags, holding her beloved straw doll.

While we played, we came upon a twisted tree that grew from the ceiling. Its leafless branches swayed upon the floor, as if begging us closer.

I refused it, but like a moth to a flame, Cassandra was a soul possessed. With eyes now glowing green, she reached up to the pulsating maw, climbing up a loose web of branches and into the gaping hole.

I grabbed for her, but a barbed vine whipped my cheek, and I fell backward.

The impact from the ground woke me instantly, my heart racing.

It was morning; a soft sun peeked over the cluster of trees where my trainer in visionary science, Hestia, and I had made camp.

"You were yelling in your sleep again," Hestia said. She wore a tattered old smock and a finely woven violet veil. She knelt over a boiling pot of water. "Who's Cassandra?"

My face flushed. I touched my stinging cheek, and my fingers came back with blood.

"Your dreams are getting more violent the closer we approach Seville."

"It's not Seville I fear," I whispered, hardly recognizing my voice.

She nodded slowly, then asked, "Did you know that blood has a very particular smell?" She threw a towel at me and continued, "It smells sweet."

"You think I smell sweet?"

She cocked her head to the side. A wind tickled the corners of her veil, exposing just a hint of the two black holes beneath. "No, you smell sour."

"You there, women, it's against royal edict to practice divination without a license in this county," interrupted a loud voice. It was a man on horseback, wearing light armor. He held a saber at his side. The hilt had an engraving of a mossy moon eating a ruby sun.

I frowned and snapped, "What right do you have—"

"As the captain of the county brigade, it is my sworn duty to uphold the law."

I was about to speak, but Hestia held up her hand, silencing me. She smiled at the captain and said, "You look weary, captain. Why don't you have a seat, and I will read your fortune. I am Hestia, Mistress of Visionary Science, and this is Ida, my apprentice."

"I won't spend my coin on your blathering palmistry." He stuck his nose up to Hestia, as if smelling something rotten.

"This is my gift to you, of course."

He quirked an eyebrow, then dismounted and joined her at the simmering pot. He offered his palms to Hestia. She grabbed him. He moved away, but she pulled him uncomfortably close.

"The steam—it hurts—"

"Chant *viven entalda* in your mind. It will remove the pain. Now, look into the cauldron," she murmured, pushing him closer.

He did as she bid, muttering the words until relief sprayed over his face. A smile crossed his features, then his brow furrowed. He tried to turn away, but her grip held firm, pulling him so close to the bubbling liquid his nose touched the surface.

"Make it stop," he whimpered, spit spewing from his lips.

"I said to chant *viven entalda*. Now, what do you see?"

A soft wind lifted her veil, exposing her empty sockets, windows into the darkness of eternity.

He blurted, "A… great treasure."

"And then?"

"An… even greater sacrifice," he responded, collapsing into sobs.

The wind died, and Hestia's veil lowered. She released the man and said, "You may go."

He didn't move for a moment as water splashed his cheeks and eyes, and then he pulled away, massaging his neck.

"What deviltry is this?" he asked. He looked between Hestia and me. His mouth kept twitching, just like the rabbit we hunted last night.

"It is your fate," Hestia spoke slowly, as one might to a child.

He frowned. "This is just a farce. I should have known the moment I came here—women working," he scoffed and added under his breath, "*Soothsaying* women at that. Clear out of here before sundown, or I will see you two hanged for the unlawful use of divination."

"Don't worry, we were just about to go," Hestia said. She kept her head leveled with his as if she really could see him.

The man faltered, then, clearing his throat, walked stiffly to his horse, and rode south.

"We must leave," I said.

Hestia turned to me and smiled. "He is not a threat. Come here. I need to be sure what I saw was correct."

I didn't move at first, but the steam, rising out of the pot, traced around my wrists and neck and beckoned me forward.

I knelt on the opposite side of the cauldron and lowered my head below the surface. There was just enough room for my face to submerge, with our cheeks touching beneath the smoldering firewater. It took every ounce of my strength not to jerk away.

"*Viven entalda*—" I gurgled.

Hestia interrupted, "You must learn to envoke *viven entalda* without moving your lips."

I tried to think the words, but I lost focus.

"Concentrate, Ida," she murmured, pushing me so my nose brushed against the metallic bottom. The heat seemed to scald my cheeks and boil my eyes. She held my head down as I writhed beneath her. Had I not been blessed with her protection, I wouldn't have reemerged with a fully formed face, but I knew I would; I always did.

"Concentrate," she repeated, but I couldn't. Pain was my everything, striking and spitting at my cheeks, swallowing up my soul. "Ida," she pushed, and then the mantra spun from her lips, causing the pain to vanish all at once, and a nothingness swept over my sight.

The nothingness became a dilapidated castle, overlooking a crashing sea.

Hestia took my hand. Her veil had lifted, revealing two dark brown eyes. She led me through a breached castle gate, marked with a fallen family crest of a black tree. The same crest from a family in my city; I faltered. The dungeons had been one thing, but the crest made it real.

Hestia guided me over a discarded battering ram and into the keep. Once inside, a foul, sour-like odor guided us to the familiar dungeon and then the gnarled tree. The branches had sprouted bright green leaves, swaying in the windless space.

"It's beautiful." I recognized the captain's voice.

He dropped his sword and climbed the branches.

A wide cavity opened for him to enter. I expected to see his precious treasure, but instead, I saw Cassandra, reaching out for me. Her eyes were no longer luminescent green. They had returned to their pale blue.

I ran toward her as Hestia pulled me out of the pot. I fell to the ground, choking up water.

"Just as I feared. Your dreams are getting stronger for a reason. We must ride south. Quickly, let's pack up," Hestia said and stepped into the wagon.

I struggled to my feet and did as she bid.

We rode in silence as Hestia ran her fingers over an imprinted book of royal crests. "It is the crest of Alejo, the fallen family," Hestia said in a low voice. "Alejo had great promise, but the king's command destroyed them for the crime of botanical mischief. Rumors of a lost heir persist despite evidence to the contrary."

I said nothing. That family had been the reason my parents disappeared and why the city fell into chaos. I had only just escaped. I had nothing until I met Hestia.

I shook the memory from my mind and stared at the road ahead.

We traveled all night, passing Seville, and in the early hours of the morning came upon the castle that I knew too well. The air was no longer foul like my vision; rather, it was salty, like the sea. A welcome gift from my old life.

I approached the castle, excitement bubbling in my heart. I knew the dungeons like the back of my hand. I could get us to the tree with or without the sour air.

"You cannot go into the dungeons," Hestia said, placing her hand at my heart. "Only the blind can face this threat and live. Take a torch to the garden and burn the roots."

"No, I have to go down there—I have to save Cassandra." I kept my voice steady, but my heart palpitated. I saw the tree in my mind. It had no lips, but I knew it was smiling.

Cassandra would be like the many who had vanished. A small child with not even her doll for company.

"Trust me," Hestia said.

My mouth opened, ready to argue, but she had already stepped into the dungeon's darkness.

I grabbed the torch, exploring the ruins until I came upon the garden. The original entrance had been boarded up, but part of the north-facing wall had collapsed inward.

The inner perimeter displayed scorch marks that had left the garden desolate of everything other than the tree's protruding roots; these had enveloped the collapsed bricks and extended up toward the ceiling. The three longest had burrowed into the level above.

I crept toward its center, but my clumsy footfalls betrayed my presence. The roots twitched and slithered toward me. The nearest, thick like a meaty thigh, wrapped around my belly, and a feather-thin branch stretched around my neck and constricted my throat. I gasped as I dropped my light to claw at the viper-like grip. A third shot for my leg, but as I kicked it away, a dozen more branches conspired around me.

Memories of my mother and father walking into the dungeon flooded my mind. I was a child again, and my parents were rushing into the castle.

I closed my eyes, daring to breathe under the tight confines, and then my foot brushed against the torch.

I opened my eyes. The torch was still burning hot and vibrant. I punted it. The torch flew up in the air, into the center of the plant mass and set the vines into on fire.

Screams of a thousand lost voices, cut into my eardrums, spewing crimson onto my shoulders.

Four branches grabbed my hands and feet, lifting me up. Despite the flames, the tree seemed determined to take me with it. White-hot pain shot through my body, my bones cracked and separated. I screamed, momentarily forgetting myself.

"Stay with us, Ida," said a familiar voice. She was a purr beneath the screams. I snapped my head to the sound, but there was no one. And then the woman spoke again, only this time I knew it was my mother. She had the same soft intonation I cherished from childhood, "Say your mantra. The pain will go away, just like it did when we left you. You were saved, my love. Please save us."

I inhaled and tried to speak, but the root around my neck was too tight. It was like I was back in the pot with hot water burning my face. Only this time, I was alone.

A hand tickled the root around my neck. I opened my eyes, but my vision was a blur of red and black.

"My little, Ida," said my father.

The chant formed in my head, but fell away.

"Just focus."

I tried again, despite my head spinning, despite my muscles twisting and pulling. Ever since I was orphaned, I had ignored the pain—stuffed it away for strength, but today I didn't. Today, I sat with it. I accepted it as I accepted the sky was blue and the grass was green. And as I accepted it, the chant formed clear in my mind, and the torment vanished. For the first time in my life, I floated in peace.

Something cracked, and I dropped to the ground, suddenly untethered. It was Cassandra. She stood at the entrance, beside Hestia. Cassandra was sticky with sap, holding a sword, engraved with a mossy moon eating a ruby sun. She dropped the weapon beside the smoldering garden, and with the help of Hestia, they carried me back to the wagon.

We sat, none of us capable of driving. Hestia knelt over me, mumbling words of restoration. Had I the strength to push her away, I would have. I was already healed. What I needed more was sleep. Cassandra needed the healing. She seemed so much smaller outside of my dream. So much frailer. I willed her to look at me, to make some connection, but she kept her eyes on her hands. In one, she had her old doll, and in the other, she held a bright glistening emerald seed.

Lean Pickings

W. J. Lewis

The stink of the corpses never goes away. I wrap my face in rags soaked with cheap wine. Doesn't help. Makes my scars itch too.

Today, I'm lucky. The battle's only just finished. No chance for decay to take hold. Cloudy, but not rainy. This is good and bad. Good, as it makes searching the bodies more pleasant. Bad, because there's more competition. More rats searching for the best pickings. Also means the voided bowels and sticky blood aren't washed away. The rain cleans the battlefield, sometimes. Sometimes, when it rains, the dead almost look at peace.

I wrap my dirty cloak around myself as the wind bites. Not enough to blow away the stench, but enough to chill. Glad it's not sunny though. Makes the smell even worse. Invites even more flies. Small mercies.

I turn one over. Axe wound to the skull. Quick one, must have been. I scan him. Low born. Probably not worth my time. I pat him down anyway. Find a pouch around his neck. A small wedding ring. *Worthless to me, might gain me a copper.* Probably meant the world to him.

I move on. Scan wounds, bodies, faces. Mostly men. Don't think of them as people; they're meat. They did not have lives before. Nor did I, before I became this scarred flesh scraping a living from the dead. A flash of gold. A necklace. The body is female. There are a few who fight. I swallow, tongue tastes corpse-stink through the wine. I leave the necklace. I don't think of my wife, left behind in another life.

I can see Jax in the distance. *Bastard.* I hurry.

I'm lucky with the next one. Highborn. Can't see what killed him. Heart attack, maybe. Not a young man. Crow's feet 'round the eyes. Wonder what made him laugh? Nothing funny in this world that I can see. Gray in the fashionable beard. Find a nice dagger on his hip, should fetch a good price. I think about removing the embroidered waistcoat, but that will take time. Time's not on our side in this business. Not on anyone's.

This place reminds me of that.

I can see Jax, moving swiftly from body to body. I gamble and leave the highborn.

It's about speed, this game. Work quickly before the soldiers return. They don't like us Crows trying to make a dishonest living. I pick up a sword, good balance to it. A golden ring, an emerald on a necklace. Take a nice pair of boots. I'll keep those for myself. Cold weather's coming. Can feel it in my knee.

I don't see the faces as I work. Don't want to. I ignore the wounds. Try and ignore the cloying taste of rot clawing at my throat. The sun peeks from behind a cloud, makes me sweat beneath my rags. Makes the scars itch worse. I take a swig of spiced brandy from my hip flask. It's early, but whatever gets you through the day, right?

Jax plunges his stiletto into a body. Sometimes they're not quite dead. Sometimes it's a mercy. Or good business. You find one alive, and they're commoners, you get more for their corpse. More hassle than it's worth, a live lowborn. Find a live highborn, mind. Get them to a field surgeon. Sometimes get a reward. Worth a gamble, sometimes. Usually not. Usually best to just silence them.

Take what we can in this life.

It's been lean pickings today. I'd come into it with high hopes. Watched the battle, saw the lances flickering in the sunlight as the knights charged. The golden-haired Bold Lion, leading from the front. He crushed them, again. The Lizard King is fighting a losing retreat. His own people don't call him that of course. Just us. To them, he is just King Rory. To us, though... the enemy.

Couldn't help the shiver down my spine at the time. I remember it. The glory. Memories mix together. Laughter as we trained. Camaraderie as we bonded. The nervous jangle of armor. Scent of sweat. Anticipation. Waiting for the test of manhood. Knowing we were on the side of good. Fighting the aggressor. Fighting for our country. The king's coin in our pocket and the Angels of Righteousness singing hymns from our shoulders. The immortality of youth.

The feel of the urine down my legs. The frantic charging, burning muscles, bile in my throat, heart slamming in my chest. The clangor of metal on metal. The fear. The pain of blades biting into my flesh.

Pain. Fear. Horror.

I blink. Shake away the memories. Part of me still wishes I'd been down there amidst the fighting, even now. The stupid child in me. He's not quite dead. Not yet. Much as life is trying to kill him.

I look down at these ex-people, and I see what glory really is. It's shit-covered corpses in the mud of a foreign country.

I'm distracted. Mind not on the job. *Lean pickings.* Watch as Jax crows in triumph. Looks like he's having a good day. *Bastard.*

A horn blows, short sharp battlefield signal, and I react on instinct. I scramble from the battlefield, as a platoon of the King's Own appears. Can't help but admire their formation. Disciplined. Doesn't stop me sprinting for the woods.

Don't want to be caught doing my job; they call it "desecration." The dead don't care, but the living are a different story.

They move among the bodies, armor shining, transferring the still-living onto carts. Try to save as many of their own as they can. But I see how they treat the wounded enemy. Sharp steel in soft throats. Put rags on a man or dress him in armor, we're all weak flesh underneath.

Sometimes I can't see the point.

A twig cracks behind me. I turn. Jax. *Bastard.* He holds up a jingling sack. He's wearing that smile of his. Bends his face into a rat's sneer. I have to consciously unclench my hand. Does something to me, that face. Always want to smash it.

"Good day, Sir Goldheart."

He calls me that. They all do, the Crows. Mocking. They don't know how much it hurts, the reminder. Of a man I could have been. A man I never was. A man I can't be.

"Sod off, Jax." I heft my own sack—he can see it's nearly empty, and that sneer of his widens. *Bastard.* I brush past him.

"After you, my Lord," he says.

I clench my teeth and stride into the forest.

* * *

The Axe and Temptress doesn't really deserve its name. A dimly lit, flea-infested room, rotting wood filled with rotten people.

The stink here is a welcome relief from the charnel house of the battlefield, but it's still bad. Oily lamps, charred greasy meat, smoke spilling from an unswept chimney. I'm tempted to put my rag back over my face, but I don't. My scars are itching, and they need some air. The floor's sticky with spilled ale and old vomit. Stained with blood from countless knife fights. The kind of place where you're sized up as you walk in, and if you're weak you don't walk out again.

This place is home of the Crows, and their leader, Big Sal.

I walk through the taproom and nod to Millie. She just stares back. Doesn't say much, Millie. Hard as a knuckle, she is.

I walk into the backroom. Don't knock. My little rebellion. As I enter, Big Sal looks up at me. A plate of chicken bones sits by her elbow. Her jowly face is mild as she raises a black eyebrow. She's in a dangerous mood. Behind her in the gloom, Dump, her bodyguard, eases a finger away from the trigger of his crossbow.

"Could have been killed, barging in," says Big Sal. I shrug. I put my sack on the table. Her other eyebrow joins the first. "That it?"

I shrug again. There's a knock at the door behind me. I don't turn, because I don't care who it is.

"Ahh, Jax," she says, her face wobbling into a gap-toothed smile. "That looks like a large sack."

"You know what they say about a man with a large sack?" he says, swaggering past me and placing his bag on the scarred table.

"They need to see a doctor," I say.

Dump snorts in the shadows, big shoulders shaking. Big Sal doesn't crack a smile and the rat sneer on Jax's face is absent. His eyes are hard.

"Wish you'd cover your face when you come in here, Goldheart," says Big Sal. "Puts me off my food."

I shrug. Do that a lot. Don't have much to say, but people expect a response, don't they? It's better than how I want to respond. A curse or a fist or a drawn blade.

Big Sal rummages in Jax's sack, a pig after truffles. Those fat fingers rifle through the bag, and her small eyes glint like a dagger in the sun.

"Jax. Well done." She throws him a little pouch. I hear the clink of coin. "Leave us. I need to speak to Gold-heart here."

Jax frowns slightly but doesn't protest. He slinks out. Gives me a wink. *Bastard.*

There's silence. I'm in no rush to break it. Big Sal peels a boiled egg. Puts the entire thing in her mouth. Chews.

Doesn't take her eyes off me. I watch. I wait. My knee hurts. My scars itch.

"You know the deal, Goldheart. You bring me a certain amount from the corpses, and I don't have Dump throttle and throw you into the Meander."

I decide not to shrug. I'm bored of it.

"If you don't bring me anything I can use…" she puts her fat fingers into my bag. Disappointed little piggy. "Then maybe I don't have a use for you."

I imagine drawing my dagger and plunging it into the soft folds of her face, seeing how many chins I have to slice through before she stops her oinking. But what's the point? One more corpse. Two, probably. I'm no match for Dump. Not anymore. Saw him break a man's neck with one hand. Cracked it like kindling, then went back to his whisky. I shiver as I remember how daintily he sipped. I realize that Big Sal is waiting for a response. I shrug.

"You have two choices, Goldheart. Either we terminate your employment here. By which I mean we strangle you, chop you into bits, and feed you to the rats." I got that, yeah. She's not subtle, Big Sal. Effective, though. Does what she says. "Or… I have a job for you."

"What is it?" I say.

"Does it matter?" she asks.

"I'm not a—"

"You're whatever I say you are. That's what you signed up for. When we pulled you from the muck, fixed you up all nice, gave you gainful employment."

Wish I'd died in the mud. With all the others.

"You're not a knight anymore, Goldheart." Don't I know it. Never was much of one. "But before you protest— you're on protection duty. Won't have to do no killing. Jax will do the blade work."

I nod. It's going to be another great night working with my favorite scumbag.

* * *

Me and Jax wait in the gloom of the alleyway. He's shaking his hands nervously, passing a coin from hand to hand. Long, lean fingers, like a musician's. Clean nails. How does he manage that?

"Stop it," I say.

"Make me," he says. But he puts the coin away. His foot starts tapping.

Across the road from us is a grand house. We can see the guards from here. Alert. Smart-looking. Can almost smell the wealth on them. I know the scent of their polished helms, the creak of their oiled leathers, the sound that their neatly greased swords leaving their scabbards. Memories of another life threaten to overtake me, and I roll my shoulders.

Focus. The grounds of the mansion are large. We scouted around, me and Jax. Took a while. Family crests and flags all over the place. Gules and Or, with a proper stag rampant over a saltire shield. Not one I recognize. Big Sal told us there'll be a gate open in the gardens, after the change of the guard.

We wait.

The evening mists arrive, and the chill in the air deepens. I wrap my cloak closer. The rain begins, gently pattering on helmets as the guards stand motionless. Well trained. I nod in approval. I tilt my face up to the heavens. The moisture stops the itching of my scars for a blessed second or two.

It's time. The guard begins to change. We sidle round to the gardens. Jax creeps to the door, silent as a weasel. Opens it. No creak. Beckons me over. I slide through the downpour, back hunched, half expecting a cry, a shout, an arrow in the back.

I make it to the door.

The drizzle patters on the greenery. I breathe in. Fresh earth, vibrant plants, and an orangery nearby. I just breathe. Realize Jax is looking at me, greasy hair plastered to his face. I snap out of it, and we creep, avoiding the gravel pathways.

Through the servants' quarters, up the stairs to the left, second floor, along a corridor, third door to the right. Our target will be in there. Alone. Sleeping. A simple job. Just draw hard steel across soft flesh. Sever a soul from its body. Get paid in coin.

My scars begin to itch again.

We arrive at the landing of the second floor. I peek down the corridor. A painting hangs on the wall, something from the school of Chebardier. All small points of color that add up to one image. Fashionable a few years back. It's a family portrait.

I don't recognize the man. The boy must be seven or so. Handsome boy. I look at the woman, and my breath catches.

Jax tugs on my arm and makes his way down the corridor. He has his knife drawn. He moves confidently. We were told there would be no guards.

I follow him. My heart begins to thump. I can taste the sick in my throat that always comes with adrenalin. I want to scratch my face, tear away the scars, reveal whatever's underneath.

Jax is at the door. He opens it and slips in. I follow. I see him, a silhouette over the bed. The curtains are open. The rain has stopped. The clouds have cleared. The moon shines in. Moonlight settles over the bed and over blonde hair, with some streaks of gray.

A flash of memory.

No time for it.

Jax is raising his knife.

I step to him, one, two, three steps, put my hand over his mouth, plunge my dagger into his body, once, twice, three times. Just beneath the ribs. He jerks under me. I lower him to the ground by the bed.

I look at the woman. Her eyes are open, horrified. She takes a deep breath. I put my hand over her mouth, bury her under my weight. She fights, but she's not strong. Her smell hits me like a lance point.

"Don't scream," I whisper. She doesn't.

My wife lies beneath me for the first time in a lifetime.

Not my wife anymore, of course. That was a different life. I was a knight back then. A man of honor. Not a corpse robber, burglar, murderer.

My scars itch.

She looks at me. I look back. I see the dawning recognition in her eyes. Maybe she recognized my voice. The only thing that hasn't changed, maybe.

"Hugo? Is that you?" Tears come to her eyes. Mine are wet, too. But it's just the scar tissue, or the rain. Sure. She speaks again. I remember that voice. I hear it in my dreams. Awake, clutching nothing. "I… thought you'd died."

I did.

I take one look at her, fix her face in my mind. Then I walk away.

I leave Jax's corpse on the floor.

Don't even search it.

The Blackest Death

E.G. Thompson

Southwest France, 1348

The village had a few names, depending on who was asked. *Eau Bénie*[1] to those who believed the tale that the waters had healed the first settlers. *Terre Fertile*[2] to those who had come after, and believed the very land beneath their feet was blessed with bounty. To many who passed through, it was simply *Répit.*[3] But to the few families who had resided there the longest, this was *Coeur de la Mère,*[4] and the villagers worked diligently to keep her heart beating.

The Heart's Daughters had practiced their craft for centuries. But for the past few generations, their practice had

1 *Blessed Water*
2 *Fertile Land*
3 *Respite*
4 *Mother's Heart*

become more secret as times changed and folk's superstitions grew. No longer was a Daughter asked to bless a goat as it was brought to slaughter—the local priest presided instead.

And when talk of the Black Death reached them in their little village, he blessed them with water instead of blood. He offered prayers instead of incantations, burned incense instead of herbs. And he grew rich while the Daughters looked on.

That didn't mean the Daughters neglected their duties. No. Now, more than ever, it was vital to continue. Despite the danger, despite fewer numbers.

Luce rested the knife in her lap, the ritual almost complete. She'd started at dawn, east of Mother's Heart, and walked the circle around the village, blessing it at every point. Posts declared that those who practice the dark arts were evil and would be burned at the stake. Luce raised her chin in defiance at these signs, and called upon the Heart Mother to keep the village safe, for she'd heard of the *Mort Noir*[5] and knew it would take vigilance and sacrifice to protect her loved ones.

"And with your Heart in mine, I call upon your grace to bless us once more, protect us from the Black Death, and deliver us through this time." Luce opened her eyes and exhaled, relieved to see that the faint, shimmery Veil hadn't tarnished, hadn't started to fade in the slightest.

The rising sun in the east warmed her face as she began the invocation. It was with hope she lifted the small knife and slit the rabbit's throat, then pulled the knife down over its belly.

She was troubled by last night's dream. In it, the Veil surrounding the village, invisible to all but the Daughters, had unraveled, and the darkness it held at bay descended as leaves and petals blew in the wind. When she woke, she looked across the yard. A young rabbit met her eye: the first life of the day.

She'd flung out her hand and snared it with her Heart's Gift, bestowed upon her by the Heart Mother herself, a gift that strengthened and concentrated Luce and the other Daughter's magical powers. She could feel the rapid life beat in the small

5 Black Death

body as it sat frozen until Luce had walked over and grabbed it by the back of its neck. She had needed it alive.

Steaming guts fell into the grass and Luce closed her eyes.

It was Mother's tongue that moved in Luce's mouth, as she recited the spell, the ancient words so worn that they almost fell apart as they flowed between her teeth.

If Luce was asked to tell anyone what the words meant, she wouldn't be able to say. They were an intent, a feeling—*protect, heal, become*. A will that transcended the words, useless without her Heart's Gift.

With a practiced motion, she wiped her knife in the grass, cleaning off much of the blood and gristle borne from the sacrifice.

Her knife cleaned, she placed her hands gently on the grass and pulled them away, and let the bloody grassprints paint her palms.

The pattern spoke to her, like tea leaves in a cup. Wisps of brown hair fell into her eyes as her brow furrowed, and the relief she'd felt just moments before faded. In its place, foreboding grew. The message was clear:

End.

The dream, her palms, even the rabbit's entrails, all pointed to an end.

The Black Death had passed by their village thus far. Despite the Daughters' efforts, their vigilance, their prayers, their Heart's Gift; would it still claim their home?

Luce peered at the shimmer once more and lifted her hand to it. Her bloody fingers caressed it as if she held the most delicate lace. The veil held.

She glanced to the side and her eye caught on a bunch of wild deadnettle. Alone, deadnettle would not harm the veil. But combined with other herbs…it was possible. With a snap of her fingers, Luce burned the deadnettle, but it did little to ease the blossoming doom in Luce's stomach. It was with heavy feet she turned north.

It was time to visit the Crone.

* * *

Luce was the Maiden, *la Vierge.*[6] In times past, there were a handful of Maids amongst the Daughters. Now, Luce was the only one. But she was not entirely alone. They had but one Mother and one Crone now.

She knocked on the Crone's door and waited, hands held loosely in front of her belly. She would not be happy to be woken so early, not after holding vigil through the night, as was her custom.

"*Vierge,*" she croaked after the door creaked open. Her black, sunken eyes pierced Luce, who bowed her head and held out her bloody palms. The Crone recoiled when she read what was on them, and opened the door for Luce.

"I am sorry to wake you, *Grand-mère,*[7]" Luce said. She made her way to the kitchen and began measuring herbs for tea. "All the signs, my dream, the entrails, even... my heart, all say the same: *end.*"

"You did well to come to me, *Vierge,*" the Crone said, reaching for the clay cup Luce held before her. "I knew this was coming."

"You knew?"

The Crone peered at her, into her, before sliding her eyes to the small fire. She nodded.

"When I was *Vierge,* my *Grand-mère* told me I would be the last Crone. She said it while in a fever-dream, sick on her death-bed, but I knew it to be true."

"*Grand-mère,* if you knew, why didn't you ever tell us?" Tears pierced Luce's eyes as the truth struck her heart.

"Would you, or *Mère*[8] Marie, have attended your duties if you knew the end was coming, knew it was all for naught?"

The Crone sipped her steaming tea as Luce contemplated the question.

<hr>

6 *The Virgin*
7 *Grandmother*
8 *Mother*

Being a Daughter had been her whole life. A whole, secret life filled with power she'd never even dreamed of had she been an ordinary village girl.

She'd done great things with her Heart's Gift, healed many people who would've otherwise suffered and died. She'd protected Mother's Heart, just like Marie had, just like the old women before her. There had never been any doubt in her purpose—the taste of *Grand-mère's* distrust was sour in her mouth.

"I would have, *Grand-mère*," her voice wavering, "had you trusted us."

The Crone hissed as she sat back on her stool, clanking her cup down; Luce was surprised it didn't crack.

"You do not question me, *Vierge*!" she spat. "You do not know what carrying this burden has done to me. To know that we three would be the last. That in our time, Mother's Heart would die, and us with it. I would not wish this burden—this curse—on anyone. It was not distrust, but to spare you, you and Marie."

Luce put her head in her hands, not caring that her tears mixed with the dried blood, dirtying her face.

"Come now, *Vierge*—dry your tears, clean your face." The Crone handed Luce a damp scrap of cloth. "You will go to Marie and tell her to meet us outside the Womb tonight, after moonrise. We will pray to the Heart Mother and ask for her guidance."

Luce did as she was told.

* * *

"Luce, *ma chère*,[9] what brings you by?"

Marie, the Mother, stood in her doorway with two small boys peeking around her skirt, and a baby girl snuggled happily into her breast.

"Ill tidings, I'm afraid," Luce replied. "May I come in?"

"Of course."

The Daughters did not often fraternize in the open, not in recent times when the nosy priest often had his eyes out, so

9 *My dear*

it had been many months since Luce had seen Marie. Months since little Clara had been born.

"She's grown so much," Luce said, smiling at the babe.

"She has!" Marie replied, beaming. "One day, she will be a fine Daughter."

Luce couldn't hide the pain that flashed across her face. Marie looked into her eyes, sensing the deep grief in Luce's heart.

But the words of what she had seen that morning wouldn't come. Instead, Luce said, "The Crone has bid us to meet at the entrance of the Womb tonight, after moonrise. Will you join us?"

"Yes, after I get the boys to bed." She gazed down at the sleeping baby. "I'll need to bring Clara."

Luce nodded. "*Grand-mère* won't mind."

She wanted to tell Marie everything, but there were two little pairs of ears nearby who heard and understood more than they let on. Even if she could bring herself to utter the words that weighed on her heart, she shouldn't.

"Tonight, then," Luce said, moving toward the door.

Marie's brow furrowed as she took in everything that Luce didn't say. She gripped Luce's arm just as she stepped outside the house.

"Tell me one thing," she whispered to Luce. "I can smell your fear and taste your dread, it hangs over you like a cloud. It's something we cannot stop, isn't it?"

Luce pinched her eyes shut and managed a single nod before she left, tears streaming down her face.

* * *

Outside Mother's Heart, down a faint track, was a glen few dared approach. The abundance of flora and fauna within tempted only the most desperate of hunters, and they never tarried long. Something about the copse made their hearts race and their skin damp.

In the center was a small stone circle. Within the stones, so worn they were almost flush with the earth, grew three ancient trees. Their spidery arms reached toward the moon, hiding the small opening in the ground between them. Into this opening walked the Crone, the Mother, and the Maid.

It was barely big enough for a woman to ease in sideways, but passed the entrance, it expanded on the long, slight decline. The Crone muttered an incantation and a ball of fire burst in her hand to light the way.

The cave was cold, and the air was stale, but the three women felt nothing but reverence. Even baby Clara held her little tongue.

As they crossed the threshold, the Womb seemed to sigh as the Daughters entered the sacred space. The tunnel had been chilly and damp, but the Womb was warm and safe, a place only the Daughters had ever entered. The Crone spread her hands to ignite the surrounding torches. The skulls of previous Daughters, placed in carved out recesses, smiled down upon them, dozens of ancient faces shining in the firelight. Dried flower crowns decorated the most recently deceased. With a gentle caress, Luce laid a fresh flower adornment atop her own grandmother's brow, who had passed long ago.

A crude stone statuette overlooked the Womb, its altar covered with dried flowers, carved wooden idols, small clay pots, and an assortment of treasures that women of simple means would hold dear: a comb, seashells, a silver ring.

Luce placed a woven mat beneath the Crone as she sank to her knees in front of the stone figure, then did the same for Marie. As the Maid, she was not afforded this comfort, so she slowly eased herself to the hard, cold floor behind them.

"Heart Mother!" the Crone began. "The signs you've given us tell us this is the end. Do we accept your acquiescence, which goes against everything you've taught us? If so, we are ready to give our lives now. We only beseech you to give us a sign of your will."

The Crone opened a pouch of herbs into a small brazier in front of her and ignited it with a wave of her hand. The herbs instantly smoldered, and the Crone inhaled deeply while Marie and Luce chanted.

Luce was forbidden from peering at the Heart Mother in her glory, but she could still hear the Mother's soothing voice, bouncing around the Womb as if a thousand women whispered, their words stretched across the cavern.

"Daughters," she said, "my sight grows dim. My bones crumble and my spirit is in tatters. You have kept me alive long enough."

"Dear Mother," the Crone cried, grief splintering her voice. "What would you have us do?"

"Leave." The torches flickered as a spectral wind danced around the cavern. A chill worked its way up and down Luce's back, and she squeezed her eyes shut even harder.

"Leave this place, for the Veil grows thin. The dark scission was long foretold to rend asunder the holy Veil. Deadnettle, thistle, primrose are all that are needed to invoke the curse."

But the Daughters are the only souls who know this, Luce thought.

"Leave your Heart's Gift here at my feet, dear Daughters, and flee," the Heart Mother continued.

"Flee!" bounced around the cavern, echoed by every skull.

The torches and candles went out as the Heart Mother left them. It was Marie who reignited them, for the Crone sat motionless.

Luce went to her side, fearing she had died, but the tears running silently down her wrinkled face said otherwise.

"*Grand-mère,*" Luce said softly, cupping her hand to the old woman's face and gently wiping it with her sleeve. "What should we do?"

The Crone didn't reply. It wasn't until after Clara awoke with a cry, that she said, "The time of our Heart Mother is over."

"It goes against everything she's taught us," Marie said. "Do we obey her, as we've always done, or stay true to our vocation and do our best to thwart this curse?"

"That is what we are here to decide." The Crone looked around the cavern. "I feel she is gone. This place... it is empty now. She will never return."

"I don't think I can flee," Marie said. "I would never forgive myself for abandoning my home, these people. Even if they don't deserve our protection."

"I feel the same, Marie," Luce said. "I have to do what we've always been taught to do."

"Then we are all in agreement. Our final act in the name of the Heart Mother is defiance. May she forgive us."

One by one, they sank to their knees in front of the altar. Luce could feel her Heart's Gift deplete from her as if she'd slit her wrist and let her life drain onto the stone floor.

The walk out of the Womb was somber. Fire in the Crone's palm was weak—each of them still had their natural magic gift, but the strength the Heart Mother had left them.

After they left the opening, the Crone placed her hand on the stone. A hum filled the air until it cracked and crumbled, closing the entrance forevermore. They did not speak as they made their way back to the village.

At the top of the track, the priest waited. He did not speak to them, nor did they speak to him, but his eyes followed them as they walked. They knew he'd waste no time telling the magistrate that he had seen them exit the woods at dawn.

Luce's mother met her at the door, a firm line across her face. It wasn't that she disapproved of Luce's vocation, but it was illegal. Her mother had abandoned her gift when it was outlawed to protect her children, as many other Daughters had. She had begged Luce to abandon it too. Outwardly, she disapproved of her rebelliousness, but inwardly, she admired it. But the defiance Luce usually felt was gone—in its place, resolve.

"*Maman,*[10] the village is in danger," she said quietly, so as not to wake anyone. "Papa must take you all as far from here as he can. Please."

"You know as well as I, daughter, that he will not leave."

For the first time in years, Luce embraced her mother.

"*Maman,* please." With the remnants of her Heart's Gift, she willed her mother to find a way to convince her father

10 *Mother*

to leave. Or, failing that, to find the strength to gather up her brothers and sisters and leave without him. "The Heart Mother has left us—she told us to flee. I will do all I can, but it won't be enough. You will die here if you don't leave, all of you will."

Her mother nodded.

The Crone, the Mother, and the Maid had agreed to a plan before departing the Womb. The Crone and the Maid would keep vigil on the Veil until dawn. Now that the sun was in the sky, Luce had a job to do.

Despite her fatigue from staying awake the night before, she packed her little bag with food for the day, threw her shawl over her head, and left to guard the Veil.

* * *

Semi-lucid, Luce could feel the end approach. Fire and death danced at the edge of her consciousness as she felt the Veil tear. Instantly alert, she ran toward it, straight across a field completely oblivious to the damage her feet wrought to the crops in her way. Her heart pounded as she ran. She spied a girl with an armful of herbs—deadnettle, thistle, primrose—walking toward the village, utterly unaware of what the plants she carried had just done.

Was it pure bad luck that the girl had unknowingly carried the exact combination that could undo the Veil? Or was the curse influencing her?

"Girl," Luce shouted, "what do you carry in your arms?"

The girl was taken aback by Luce's tone, the wild look in Luce's eyes, her flushed face, and muddy hem. Instead of answering, the girl fled.

Using her own blood to mend the torn edges, she smeared her lifeforce across the Veil. So focused was she on repairing the damage, she did not hear the villagers approach.

"I knew it!"

Luce snapped her head around to see the village priest and the local magistrate, shackles in hand; the girl with the herbs was a few paces behind him, her eyes locked firmly on the ground.

"Consorting with the Devil in the light of the Lord's sun? You dare blaspheme in such a way?"

The magistrate grabbed her by the wrist and hauled her after him. Luce tried to use her Heart's Gift to sway him, to get away, but there was nothing left.

All too soon, she found herself bound and escorted to a jail cell.

The blood on her hands dried. It read, *Fin.*[11]

* * *

"*Vierge,*" a voice hissed through the metal bars. "*Vierge!*"

Luce woke. Her head pounded, but she was able to see that the Crone had come for her. How long had it been? Without their Heart's Gift, the Crone had stolen the cell keys from the sleeping magistrate.

"The Veil was torn," the Crone said as she opened the door.

"I know..." she explained, "I failed to seal it."

"Then it's time for you to go," the Crone said. "You and Marie both, you will go. Tonight. I will remain."

Luce wanted to protest, but she could tell by the way the Crone held her head, by the weight of her voice, there would be no arguing.

Once outside, Luce could just make out a pyre in the moonlight, and her heart stopped.

"Did they mean to burn me?" she asked.

"Yes," the Crone replied. "The plague is here. The fool priest said you must die in order to cleanse the village." The Crone gripped Luce's arm. "Many are already stricken."

Words failed her, so Luce placed her hand over her heart and bowed deeply to the Crone, who nodded in return.

11 End

Luce made her way home, finding it abandoned. She whispered a prayer to the Heart Mother, thanking her for protecting her family. She packed a few things before leaving.

On the way to Marie's house, Luce heard the muted whine of a donkey. She found him behind a neighbor's house, tied to a post, his muzzle wrapped in rope.

"If you hold your tongue," she whispered to him, "and do as I command, I will free you."

The donkey met her eye, shining in the moonlight, and she knew he understood.

A name came to her—"Benoît," she blessed him. Carefully, she unwound the rope and gently rubbed the deep rivets in his flesh.

"Come on, then, Benoît," she whispered.

He followed.

Marie met her outside, sleeping babe in her arms, and her two wide-eyed, silent boys standing on either side, clutching her skirt.

"Roul won't come," she whispered. "In fact, he forbids me to leave. He's asleep now."

Luce knew what that meant—she had drugged him. She began to load up Benoît, with the baskets and bundles Marie had brought outside. Then, she helped the boys on Benoît.

They walked north for several miles until they came across an empty hovel just as the sun was rising. Marie cried, in relief and grief, when she laid eyes on the freshly dug graves behind the house. There was nobody here to claim it.

The dawn revealed a pillar of smoke to the south. Marie and Luce sank to their knees and clutched one another as their loss washed over them—the Crone had been burned at the stake in Luce's place.

The last Crone was dead.

And *Coeur de la Mère* would follow her soon.

* * *

Several weeks later, a traveler passed the little hovel that Luce, Marie, and the three children now called home.

"What news of *Coeur de la Mère*?" Luce asked him, offering a cup of well water.

"*Eau Bénie*? The village south?" At Luce's nod, the man shook his head and looked at the ground. "Do not go there, mademoiselle," he said over his shoulder as he rode away. "There is nothing there but death."

Marie looked at Luce and saw the same resolve she'd seen in the Crone's worn eyes. There would be no convincing Luce not to go. Besides, Marie knew it was the right thing to do, even though it was dangerous. All she could offer were prayers.

Luce left Marie and the children at dusk. She mounted Benoît and headed south, laden down with dried herbs and kindling.

As she passed the town's sign, the admonition of witches was replaced with a red painted cross, indicating quarantine. Luce could see that the man hadn't lied: bodies were piled haphazardly, and many lay where they'd fallen. Even beneath the mask she wore, she could smell the death and rot. And at the center of the village, where they'd left her, the Crone's bones sat charred and broken in the middle of the blackened pyre.

Luce stepped into the remains of the pyre. Her fingers trembled as she picked up the Crone's skull and placed it in her bag.

Beginning in the center of the village, Luce used her herbs, kindling, and some spirits she came across to start a fire at the priest's house. Then, she slowly moved in a spiral igniting every house, every pile of bodies she came across until the entire village was alight. Strangely enough, the fire stopped at the place the Veil used to end.

With the power of the full moon, Luce could feel her dormant magic resurge, and with that swell she urged the fires to burn higher, hotter, and fiercer.

For hours, Luce watched it all burn. With her mask off, the heat blistered her face. But she didn't turn away. She would witness the death of *Coeur de la Mère*.

By the time the dawn rose, the village was smoldering. Blackened stone and charred bone were all that remained.

It was time.

Luce followed the faint track down to the sacred wood. The trees still stood, still guarding the Womb. The leaves whispered to Luce as she took the Crone's skull out of her bag and nestled it into the rubble that was once the entrance to the place that held so many memories, so many souls of the Daughters who had come and gone before her.

"You were right," she whispered to the Crone, whose presence she felt. "You were the last one."

She brought her lips to the blackened bone to bestow a farewell kiss. Even though her Heart's Gift was spent, she still sank to her knees to offer the invocation for the final passage.

And when she was done, she placed a crown of flowers upon the Crone's brow.

Come and in My Chamber Lye

H.R.R. Gorman

"I'll get a job tamarr-ah," his words slurred from a night of heavy drinking. "My poor head's still a-hurtin' this morn'."

The baby was crying again. She did that when my breasts ran out of milk. They'd emptied faster recently, but I had no good explanation, none other than that I was just as hungry as the baby. I tucked my breasts back in my shirt and lay the baby in her reed basket. I shushed her, encouraged the poor thing to sleep with just a little hug and kiss on her forehead.

I wished I'd never had her.

"Maggie," my husband called again. "Maggie, git me a cup a coffee, will ya?"

"We ain't got none." I put on a bonnet made of patchwork cloth. "I've gotta get out soon. Sun'll rise in a mite, an' I've gotta put the clothes to boil so I can get 'em laid out in time."

He growled, willing to take a bad mood out on us. "I said, git me a cup a coffee."

I lifted the latch on the door and trembled. If I left, no one stood between him and the baby. No one stood between him and John or Thomas, ages five and three. John could start mucking stables for work in a year or so, but I dreaded putting a child to work when the children of people living up on the hill could afford schooling.

I stayed momentarily. The fire crackled in the hearth, smoke rose up the catted chimney. "I cain't make you no coffee. Ain't got none."

"Then go find me some," he ordered before rolling over on our bed. He coughed, grumbled, then breathed more evenly.

Hoping he was asleep, I lifted the latch and snuck out. I let the latch down quietly, then rifled through the things under the rickety lean-to. I slung a sack of new laundry over my shoulder then picked up a basket filled with small bags of ashes, hoof clippings, and bottles of chamber lye. Chamber lye was better when made from the piss of a little boy than a man, but something disturbed me about using my sons' piss when bleaching shirts. Whatever poison made the lye work, it stung the nostrils and burned the eyes.

My arms full, I wasn't able to carry a torch or something of the sort down to the riverside. The walk was about a quarter-mile, but in the darkness of the morning, I risked hurting my bare feet or stepping on a snake.

Some days I prayed for a snake and asked Yarenth, our God, to make it extra poisonous.

The scent of freshwater and trees lined the path. The early morning was quiet, as only the washerwomen like me and some of the fishermen were out on the river this early. I made my way around some trees and found my kettle, the coals still holding some heat and flame from where I'd left them last night.

I dropped the new laundry next to the pot.

I pulled yesterday's whites from the soaking pot using a long stick. I brought it over to a stone in the river where I would rinse out the chamber lye and beat out the dirt.

Just after my whites slopped onto the rock, a voice called out from the shore, "Mrs. Farthing! Mrs. Farthing, is that you?"

It was a woman, one whose voice was anathema to the respectable ladies of the little town. It was Esther Redd, who everyone knew was the town whore even if they didn't speak it aloud. Whores made witch Bargains with multiple men, assuming the stories were true. Witches sacrificed virtue for sin, and the Bargain turned sin into magic.

And here I was, beating urine-soaked shirts in the river and going home to desperation and hunger. I felt dirty even in a witch's presence.

I folded a shirt so the buttons wouldn't crack when I smacked it with a stick. I'd take a whore witch's money just like anyone else's. "Yes," I answered, "I'm Mrs. Farthing."

"I need some dresses washed, and I heard you do a fair rush job."

Dresses? She owned multiple dresses? Good God, was I in the wrong line of work? Of course not—my husband would kill me if I wasn't "faithful." Lord Yarenth would damn me for immoral Bargains.

I beat the shirt with my stick. "Sure. What's it to ya?"

"Three dresses. I'll pay you well. In a couple days I'll have another few. Is it alright?"

I turned the shirt, beat it again, rinsed it in the river, beat it once more. "A nickel a dress, knowin' what flouncy messes you wear. Eight cents if ya want all them petticoats."

"I'll tell you what I'll do," she shuffled around in her purse. "A nickel upfront for each, and I'll give you a dime when I pick them up."

A dime—one more penny than she owed me. "Pah," I said, spitting downriver after. "I ain't acceptin' no charity from you."

"It's not cheap I need," she said. "It's quiet. As Mr. Farthing is regularly inebriated, I thought you might need money. I hoped I might buy your silence."

I put the first shirt to the side. I needed that extra penny. "What kind a silence?"

"Washing this many dresses means increased…" she coughed, "… increased business. I got word the war front is coming this way, and one side or the other will make camp here. Soldiers make good customers, you know."

For her and for me. It was a good tip. "I'll take yer deal. Slang yer stuff o'er by the fire, an' I'll git to it soon's I can."

Her nickels clinked against a stone on the shore. "Thank you, Mrs. Farthing."

* * *

Two days later, I changed my daughter's diaper, fed her the tablespoon of milk I'd made, and kissed my boys' foreheads as they slept. I lifted the handle in the dark, thankful my husband was still out from the prior night's drunken stupor and hoped I'd get to eat today. My poor Emmeline, sweet child, was suffering as I couldn't produce enough food. Children shriveled away so fast, too.

I picked up my laundry and supplies, then ran to the riverside. Esther was already there, waiting by my fire. Even in the dim firelight, I noticed her face wasn't yet painted for the day. I handed over her package. "Count 'em if ya want, but all them petticoats are here. Bleached an' all."

Esther withdrew the promised dime from a purse. "My gossip was right about the war—I heard officers kicked townspeople out of their homes in order to quarter their soldiers."

"Means more shirts to wash for me." I pulled today's whites from the soaking pot then tossed them onto my rock. Four days since the Lord's day, and already my joints ached. My shoulders cracked as I put the stick back down. "Kin I ast ya somethin'? Ain't 'propriate, but I wanna know."

Esther held her clothes to her chest. "I can't guarantee I'll answer."

"You make any Bargains with yer fellas for magic?"

She lifted her chin. "Any woman would. The job is dangerous, and I need Bargains to replenish my magic and rid myself of disease."

I nodded. "Just wonderin'."

She cleared her throat. "You already thought I was going to the Seven Devils' hell. I know what people think of me; they make it clear."

I laughed, clucked. "Well, I jus' hope ya ain't livin' hell right now. Lookit me, leavin' my children home an' comin' down here to soak clothes in stale urine and beat 'em with a stick. We might still both go to hell, and here I am, not gettin' a thing outta life now. No nice dresses like you got."

"I think it's honorable you're trying to work virtuously while Mr. Farthing is such a layabout." She removed three nickels from her pocket. "Here. I left three more dresses by the fire. When I come to pick them up, I'll probably have another batch. And... Mrs. Farthing, have you've eaten recently?"

I furrowed my brow, but she probably couldn't see me do it in the dark. "What's that s'posed ta mean?"

"You're very thin. Your boys are wasting away, and you're breastfeeding. I had thought you were doing okay, but I saw how much rotgut Mr. Farthing had with him the other night. Is even a red cent of what you make coming to you?"

I held my tongue.

"If you wish," she said, "I could pay you in barter. Coffee, flour, a bit of meat."

I turned to the creek where my white clothing waited for the intolerable, painful beating. She followed me to the river. "He'll know if I start slackin'. We eat enough to keep us goin', and I reckon it's better than... than..."

"Than whoring?"

I beat the clothing. I sort of liked Esther, and I knew why she did what she did. I just didn't want to admit I was afraid of him killing me for stepping out of line. I couldn't admit that I didn't love him, that I was jealous of her freedom. What would she think of me?

She gathered her skirts and stepped into the river.

"There's a way I think I can help." She put her fingers on my shoulders and kneaded. Her fingers tingled like tiny strikes of lightning. My muscles jerked underneath the power of Esther's magic, but it was sensual, kind, invigorating. It felt so right that I wished she'd never release me.

"You don't need to work so hard at this," I said. A pop in my back made me groan with delight.

"It's not hard. Magic's a... a quiet exercise. It's a relaxation of the soul until it releases from the body and roams free in a world hidden between cracks in our world. There are things in these cracks, like tiny, rejuvenating lightning bolts. Like horses, snakes, or mice. All it takes to retrieve things from the other world is sin and, sometimes, a physical sacrifice to the world."

She pressed with her thumb, causing her energy to course through me. "There was no sacrifice for this little pleasantry."

When she let go, I rotated a shoulder. No cracking. I sat, dumbfounded. I couldn't see that kind face as scary anymore, not when she'd spent some of her magic on me.

"Thank you," I said. "Ya don' need to bring me that dime next time, if ya don' wanna."

She smiled. "I'll want to. You've been nice to me, and that's more than most ladies give me in this town. I'll see you in a few days."

* * *

I returned home. My muscles ached. The soldiers had been in town for two weeks, and there was no sign they'd leave. I'd worked through two Lord's days of rest, and the work had been necessary. The price of food rose since the young men ate, drank, or stole everything in sight.

I could keep working as long as Esther caressed me with magic. I sighed. Esther—so beautiful. An angel with a Bargain and magic to ease the pain of aching joints, with soothing fingertips and a calm voice.

I dropped my new laundry under the lean-to and felt Esther's dime in my pocket. Perhaps I could buy a little beef, maybe even get a touch of sugar. No—sugar was too much, especially when I could buy some rice to starch the soldiers' clothes. I'd charge a little extra for that.

I lifted the latch and pushed the door open. Dark when I'd left, dark when I arrived.

My husband stirred. A pewter cup fell on the ground from where it'd set next to him on the bed, and he grumbled. "Ya ne'er brought me no coffee, wench."

This had gone on for dangerously long—weeks. I hoped he didn't remember how long it'd been. "Didn' have no money to buy no grounds."

"Ya tellin' me I ain't workin' hard 'nuff for ya?"

"No," I answered, voice quieting. "Just sayin' we's outta money and ain't got no coffee." I hurried over to the crib where I'd placed my daughter that morning; it smelled horrid, since obviously my husband wasn't going to help change a diaper. It wasn't a man's work. I grabbed a clean napkin, then untied the old.

He grabbed me by the arm. "You cain't 'sult me like that. I tell you go get me a coffee, I 'spec you get me a coffee."

"I'll get you coffee next time."

He shook me, and I let go of the wet diaper. It fell on the dirt floor, just missing my foot.

"Where'll you git the money next time?" He shook me harder. "You said we's outta money."

I drew the pennies I'd made from my pocket. Seven pennies. "Washin'," I said. "But food's so 'spensive now with them soldiers 'ere."

He took every penny, put them in his pocket, and tossed me against the crib. "Thinkin' y'er better 'n me, just 'cause I ain't got a job nor any land. I'll spen' this money how I want, an' you kin just starve. Way you treat me..."

The dime in my pocket weighed heavy. Thank Lord Yarenth that a single dime couldn't jangle.

I bent to the floor and picked up the diaper. The watery stool smelled worse than normal. My eyes welled up with tears as I took the diaper outside. With nothing solid to toss from it, I threw it in the bucket to be cleaned the next day.

I grabbed up another rag with which to wipe her. Her legs were stiff, like she was fighting me as I cleaned. I lifted them to get better vantage, but her back lifted with the legs.

I noticed her feet were cold.

I put my hand to her chest, felt no breath rise or fall. Her heart was still, her mouth stuck in a position of misery.

I shook my head. "No," I said. "No, Emmeline, no—"

"What you sayin', woman? My head's hurtin'. Shut up."

"She's dead! My God, she's dead!" I fell to my knees and sobbed. I cried into my hands, shook. I'd failed her. I'd not wanted her, wished she'd never been born, many times. Many times.

Had this been my fault?

Why did Lord Yarenth want to punish me so? Did he kill her for my awful wish?

"Bury 'er, why don' ya, if y'er so good at workin' without a man." He spat at me, the tobacco-laced saliva landing on my neck. "It was just a girl."

"She's yer baby girl, too." I shivered. If I had the strength, I would've killed him. "We ort ta go get a preacher, bury 'er right."

"Cost money, that does, an' we'd 'ave bought some damn coffee already if we had any money. Now git, go bury 'er. Don' need a deep grave for a baby." He went to the door, unlatched it, and waved a few of the pennies. "I'm getting' somethin' to drink."

And he left me crying with the corpse and two starving boys.

* * *

Esther sat on the riverbank while I beat on a shirt and rinsed the chamber lye from the whites. She put both hands over her face, shook her head. At last, she lowered them.

"Sweet little Emmeline... died? Oh, Maggie, that's horrible. Have you gotten the priest?"

"Cain't 'ford a priest."

"I can. I've had men every night; my Bargains are strong, and I could give you the money."

I stood from my laundry and went to the shore. "No, you ain't givin' me no money. If I get money, you know where it goes? Down his gullet. Straight through to his piss an' down to the Seven Devils." I held Esther's hand in mine. "I cain't take it no more, not with 'im."

She shook her head. "I won't help kill him."

"You don't have to." I put her hand to my lips, kissed it. "Make a Bargain with me, make it salacious, an' I'll split the magic with ya."

Her hand loosed on mine, and she pulled it back without letting go entirely. "What happiness are you seeking?"

"I want my children to eat, to grow up. I wanna eat, too, and not have to feed his lust for drink." I put my hand farther up her arm, let it brush against her skin. "I need to leave 'im. I need to get my boys, and I need to run."

"I'm not fond of that plan, either."

"Why not? 'Cause you won't have a washerwoman to do yer skirts?"

She took my arm and pulled me from the shore. "Because I don't want you to leave me." She rubbed the back of my head with her magic fingers and ran through my hair.

What was this? Why did I like it; was it because she was a witch?

I leaned in closer. "I ain't sure I e're loved him."

"You might not have. You've been told your whole life you have to suffer for men, but it's not true."

I leaned closer to her. Her face was perfect in the firelight, her lips enticing.

What was I thinking? Lips? No—I couldn't! But I tugged her into a hug, my face close to hers. "Just make the damn Bargain," I said. "Please, Esther. I don't know how."

"I will, with a caveat. I will receive no magic from this Bargain." She touched my face with a hand. "Sin to magic only counts if there is sin in the first place, and I've found the trade is ineffective if one doesn't believe their actions to be a sin."

I laughed. "Not a sin? Us, together, not a sin? Yarenth laughs at ya."

"I've seen truer love between two women in a brothel than I've seen between some women and their husbands. My sin, the one that gives me magic, is sleeping with people I don't love." She wrapped her arms around me. "But I can give you magic, if you're fine with me loving you."

I buried my fingers in her dress. "Just make the damn bargain before we do this for nothing."

Her voice was breathy, sensual as she said, "With this kiss, I'll seal our souls and turn your virtue to sin, your sin to magic. Will you agree to our Bargain and become a witch by sinning with me?"

I nodded, my breath heavy. "Oh, yes," I said.

"Then may God have mercy."

I kissed her.

* * *

Esther was a good teacher, if a bit poetic about the ways of magic. She showed me those cracks in the world where all the hidden things are found and helped me learn a bit about how they worked. Maybe it was because she'd traveled through this mental maze long enough that the tunnels no longer seemed frightening, but they reminded me of catacombs or a labyrinth where the prize could elude me forever. When I projected my soul into these cracks, I usually didn't wander far for fear I would get stuck in this other world.

Magic alone, however, couldn't feed a family. I held a small sack of cornmeal from the store and some rendered fat from the hog farmer in the crook of my arms. He'd had no bacon or ham since the soldiers killed everything, so I had to make do with what little I'd got.

I smiled at the haul I'd bought before my husband's villainous whiskey tax. I'd have everything cooked and eat it with my children before he could gobble it up. Claimed he needed the strength to get a man's job... *pfft.*

Three-year-old Thomas sat gaunt in the corner of the house, eyes dark. Five-year-old John wasn't much better off. I shushed John with a finger to my lips. I grabbed the salt, a bird's egg I'd found the day before, a metal bowl, and a pan, then motioned for them to come outside.

They followed me down to the riverside where my pot of laundry sat boiling over the fire. I set everything down. "Kin you two gather some of the dandelions, spring onions, and stingin' nettles?"

Thomas nodded. "We gon' eat today, mama?"

"Yes. You gotta keep it secret, okay?"

John smiled, then dragged his brother off to search beneath the trees. Hopefully, he'd bring the right things, but I could sift through them once he came back.

I poured the cornmeal and salt into the bowl.

More importantly, though, was my first attempt at magic without Esther. The tiny bird's egg in my hand, I closed my eyes, released my soul as Esther instructed. My soul flew through mental catacombs until I found a room full of what I wanted. She said I'd get better at finding my way around this maze, but the amount of magic I held would always limit the size of what I could take.

Today, I found a room filled to the brim with large eggs. I took two and replaced them with the tiny bird's egg. I had expected to get three, but the amount of magic I'd had was too small. I'd only been a witch for a week—how was my magic weakening even though my skill improved?

I was sinning. I had to keep believing that.

I added the eggs to the cornmeal, stirred in some water, and poured it into a greased pan.

When the boys returned, I put their greens in the metal bowl with some water and salt and boiled it.

The boys ate with cheer. I should have done this before poor Emmeline starved to death.

And I wished I could be with Esther more often.

* * *

The door slammed late one night. He sang a crass tune and stumbled over both his words and his feet. I got up from the pallet on the floor, knowing he'd get violent if he thought I was in his way. He corked the empty whiskey jug, handed it to me, and crawled into bed. He belched, rolled over, and said, "Them soldiers is leavin'—most, anyway. Just leavin' a handful behind to guard the cracker line."

I didn't know what he wanted, so I sat down against the wall with his filthy jug in my hands and waited.

"I could take 'em if we just had a couple more patriots in this town, but fer now we jus' gotta keep our heads low." He uncorked his bottle and tried to drink, managing to spill a large amount on his shirt in the process. "We jus' gotta get 'em where it hurts, Maggie."

"Yes, sir." I shivered in the hopes I'd said the right thing.

"Hey, Maggie, you wanna do summat with me tamarr-ah?"

After figuring out what he'd said through his slur, I responded, "What is it?"

"After them soldiers leave, we's gonna hafta punish summun. They's a witch what slep' with all 'em, so we reckoned it's time for a burnin' once her Johns are all gone." He took a swig. "I could cast lots with the other fellas, see if I couldn' git you one a her fancy dresses."

My heart leapt into my throat, choking me.

"Knew you'd—" he belched "—knew you'd like one. Mebbe I'll sleep with ya agin, and mebbe this time you won't slop out another damn baby. Hard 'nuff fer me to keep ya an' these two useless things alive." He pointed to my boys.
I looked around for some way to kill him. He couldn't do this, couldn't threaten my love. I didn't have a kitchen knife, didn't have any cast iron skillets or pots like other people. All I had was firewood and not much of that.

"Hey," he said, "Gimme sip water, will ya?"

Water. The man pickles his insides and rots his brain with hatred for my daughter and my love, and he wants me to fetch him water?

I had followed his commands forever and obeyed the false tradition that I must love him because my parents sold me to him. Getting this water would be the last order I ever followed.

I stood, his liquor jug still in my hand. "Yes, sir. Bucket onna porch is empty—kin I take the boys as pertection while I go to the well?" Before he even responded, I moved over to the pile of straw on the other side of the fireplace and rustled the boys awake.

"Sure," he said in drunken stupor. "Giddout."

John blinked his eyes as I shook him. "Mama?"

"Shh," I said. "Daddy's tryin' a sleep, an' we gotta git water from the well."

"Aww, shucks. Why?"

"Don't ask me questions," I ordered, trying to stir little Thomas awake. He refused to get up, and out of a sudden fear, I felt for his pulse. He was still alive. I picked Thomas up, hoping he'd wake soon. "Come on. We gotta git."

John roused, rubbed some sleep from his eyes, and grabbed hold of my skirt. He followed me outside to the bucket hanging by the door, which I removed from its hook, and then to the well dug where the people nearby could access it. I sat John, Thomas, and the liquor jug down by the cover, then opened the well and lowered the bucket.

I bent to my knees to better draw the bucket and speak in a soft voice to the boys, "Now, you have to be quiet. Stay here and be quiet, no matter what you hear next."

Thomas nodded, and John gulped. He knowingly asked, "What's happening, mama?"

"I just have to go get our things, then we're leaving."

He nodded, as did Thomas. Hopefully, he knew it was necessary, even if he didn't know what had forced me to make this decision.

I picked up the bucket and the jug, then went back to the house. I walked around the corner where my boys couldn't see me, then shuffled through the lean-to where I stored my laundry. My hands gripped the bottle of chamber lye, and I drew it out from between the folds. I unstopped the lye and the empty liquor jug, then poured the evil man's soured piss inside.

I corked the half-filled jug, dipped a gourd into the bucket of water, then brought both inside the little cabin where I'd wasted the last six years of my life.

He stirred at the sound of the door. "What took ya so long?"

In my right hand was the jug, my left the gourd. "I got you a drink." I lifted the jug. "This is your rotgut poison." I lifted the gourd. "And this is water. Take your pick."

He looked at me, suspicious, then to the two jugs. "I finished that one," he said.

"Ain't empty now." I sloshed the chamber lye around so he could hear it.

He grabbed the bottom of the jug with two hands and yanked it from my fingers. "Why'd you not say so when I give it to you?" He uncorked it and, without wasting a second, tipped the jug to his lips. He swallowed without stopping.

Then he coughed, gagged, retched. The bottle fell to the ground and burst. The stringent scent of stale urine pervaded the room. "What you do to me, woman!"

He rolled over and out of the bed, then lunged at me while his breath wheezed. In his drunken state, I avoided him. He remained prostrate and shook uncontrollably. His eyes rolled into the back of his head. His mouth foamed. He coughed up vomit from his lungs.

Confident he was helpless, I walked up and stood over him. "It was chamber lye. I'm lettin' ya choke and die in your own piss and vomit, just like ya let Emmeline die in a dirty diaper." I gripped the collar of his shirt and pulled it close, even though the seizing, shaking man probably couldn't hear or understand me anymore. "I hope the Seven Devils in hell give you what you deserve." As the man's choking slowed and his dying quickened, I fished a couple of jangling dimes and three pennies from his pocket.

I left the stinking cabin to fetch my boys from the well and save Esther from what tomorrow morning held in store.

* * *

I led John and Thomas to a little house of ill repute, and I knocked gently on the door. I waited a bit before knocking again.

"Esther—Esther, it's me. Git up!"

Nothing.

I tried the door to see if the latch was held shut by something on the inside, and it gave way easily. I placed Thomas beside the door, and he looked up at me while I said to John, "You keep Thomas safe, y'hear? I'm jus' goin' inside to talk with summon, an' ya bes' keep right by this door. Unnerstand?"

John nodded. Thomas looked up at me with eyes that asked when we'd be going home, but his lips didn't move.

I entered. I heard a second set of breaths from Esther's guest, so I crept toward her rack with dresses hanging down from it. I wanted her to keep them, or have them to sell in a pinch. I picked one off the rack.

The dress squealed and squeaked—a rat, caught between some of the frilly petticoats, fell out. The soldier didn't stir even when I gasped. Heavy sleeper, it seemed. The rat scurried around the small room, not finding any better place to rest. It curled up in a corner, waiting for us to go away.

Esther sat up in bed, rubbed her lovely cheeks. Her breasts hung, plump and attractive.

I crept forward, compressing the dress to my body with one hand and put the other on her chest. I leaned in to place a kiss on her forehead. I felt magic enter me, but it was a trickle now. Kissing her had become commonplace and was no longer sin to me, especially in the face of what I'd just done.

Her eyes fluttered awake. "What are you doing here?"

"The men in town're gonna burn ya," I whispered. "Tonight, oncet the soldiers leave. We gotta git outta here now. I got my boys out by the door, an we's ready. If we go now, we kin join up with the camp followers an' be safe."

She got up from the bed, still beautifully naked, then pulled on her clothing. The rat squeaked when she moved from bed, but it had nowhere to run.

"Burn me?" she asked. "No—they've let me ply my trade for ages. They know a witch is hard to get rid of!"

"But they's mad you slep' with the enemy. It's jealousy what they's killin' ya over, not witchery." I handed her a shawl, picked up one of her dresses.

She took me by the shoulders. "You can't run with me, dear. You have two sons to take care of, and they aren't fast enough to stay ahead of a mob."

I took another dress from where it hung near her wall and bit my lip. I tried to invent a method to speed our escape, but the rat interrupted my thoughts with its infernal squeaking. Esther touched me. "You're married, Maggie. I can go, and I can send you money."

"I'm not married anymore. Not to that beast. I didn't come wake you up 'cause I wanted yer money, neither." I swallowed. "I came because I love you."

Esther's eyes welled. "You killed him?"

I nodded. "I gave him poison." My arms tightened around the dresses in my arms, wishing this dear woman didn't have to know her lover was a murderer. "Please, I had to do it. Please forgive me, Esther."

Her eyes welled, but she pushed a strand of hair behind my ear. "We both knew something like this would happen eventually, but I wish it hadn't required your actions." She kissed me on the lips. "I also love you so much that I can't make you leave your sons or carry them off just to die."

The rat squeaked.

"Gah," Esther complained. "Stupid, nasty rat. If only we could ride out on it."

I considered a rat the size of a horse, of riding it away. A rat of that size probably existed in the catacombs. For that matter, a horse probably existed in the mental maze.

"That's it!" I said, tossing the two dresses to her with a kiss to the cheek. I ran over to the corner where the rat was, then leaned down. I picked up the rat, avoiding its bite. "C'mon—let's git outside!"

I led her out, rat still trying its best to bite or scratch at me, and sat down. This would take a lot of magic, and I would be very tired after casting the spell even if it didn't work. I closed my eyes, released my soul, and searched the mental catacombs for horses.

I found it, and I placed the rat inside the tunnel.

The horse, however, wasn't easy to drag back from the horrible place it came. I whimpered as I pulled it by the mane. Some fingers on my back pressed magic into my bones, re-charging me. A kiss tingled up my neck, invigorating our bond. "Yarenth," I begged, "Please, please let love fuel the magic today. Let love be turned to magic, not sin."

A black stallion exited the void.

Esther helped me stand, kept me up.

Though I was tired, completely drained, I held onto the horse and let her help me atop it. "Git them boys," I said. "It may be a long ride, but we're all goin' away from here."

"But we've got no place to go. No home."

She blew me a kiss and collected my sons.

"It don' matter where we go. We'll be safe together."

I knew, by the blood of Yarenth, that with her I was already home.

Day of Miracles

Jonathan Reddoch

Sir Marvyn Alabaster of Gweenton Pitch hastily marched to the royal market. His path ventured through the stretch of filthy lanes laden with uneven stones and foul rivers of unmentionable fluids known ironically as Fiddler's Garden, which required careful navigation through a gauntlet of human leeches.

He first passed a blind man with his mangy wolf. The wild canine growled while the begger shook his tin cup in Marvyn's face. "Will warsh my unclean hands for a gold coin, me lord." Marvyn laughed internally at the offer, *ew*. Had the jest earned a farthing? Perhaps. But he had no time for unpleasant peasants. He had an important task to undertake. As he stepped on, the wolf nipped at his plum-colored pantaloons.

Escaping the beast, Marvyn stepped over a passed-out hag with a flagon in her hand. A thirsty black cat was licking her smiling wet face. The cat hissed a curse in ancient feline tongue at Marvyn for interloping.

Marvyn was then accosted by a crowd of child grifters, posing as a troupe of acrobats. They patted his thickly-padded attire, searching for a dangling purse. Marvyn learned long ago to keep few tokens on his person while in the company of massing miscreants.

He clutched his pearly white package closely and shook his jeweled staff in their grimy faces. "Scat, you unruly urchins!"

In response, the young rascals flipped his cape over his crinkled face and kicked his shins before running away shouting, "Fancy pants! Fancy hat! Fancy coat! Fancy fat!" One young girl fled performing cartwheels, and a boy did a backflip, landing with an obscene gesture.

He took great offense that his slightly rotund appearance was made a point of ridicule from soiled ragamuffins. Still, he had little time to stand in the filthy street and contend with unkempt children.

He continued down the lane toward the market. It was starting to rain.

"Hello, kind gentleman," whispered a fair maiden, "would you kindly aid me?"

Marvyn was dumbstruck by the sultry voice. She stood in the alley between a seedy pub and a brothel inhabited by the least enticing harlots within the town wall. And yet, this vision before him was enchanting beyond belief, perhaps even more so considering her vile surroundings.

Clearly no mere lady in scarlet, she wore a genteel bonnet over her golden locks and a simple blue country dress. She stood astride a wooden pony-pulled cart; a wheel had come loose and she seemed in desperate need of a gentleman's assistance.

"Why, my l-l-lady," he sputtered. "Tis, but my honor alone."

She laughed. "I do declare this a day of miracles."

She led him to the cart. He bowed and pledged his loyalty, "I am but thy humble servant."

"And I am but a humble maiden," she said with a crackling cough.

"Oh no, are you stricken with the dreaded crimson influenza?" The flu had decimated the country the prior season, destroying lives old and youthful, wealthy and destitute, fair and foul.

"No, no," she smiled, "I am not yet well-acquainted with the odorous air of the tumultuous city."

"Yes, I see," he said, relieved.

He entreated her to sit upon a broken barstool while he set about to right the wheel as best he could. First, he lay down his fragile package upon an old barrel. Then he located a large beam and wedged it under the cart. He braced the other end of the bream with his shoulder and lifted with all his might. He motioned for the maiden fair to now place the wheel back onto the axel. She did so, and he lowered the beam. All was well again.

He seemed quite exhausted from the deed. And she was rapt with pleasure. So, to thank him, she offered him her favor. She pressed her lips to his, which were laced with dewdrops of heaven.

The foolish mortal sighed and grinned stupidly. "Now, I must take my package, miss, and my leave," he said, failing to seize his bundle. "I... must... hire..."

He collapsed to the ground.

The package was hers, whatever it was. Transforming to her true form, a thousand-year-old crone with a penchant for murder, mayhem, and mysticism, she carefully unwrapped the treasure.

"What do we have here," she spoke to her former pony, now revealed to be an ebony, winged donkey. "I have myself a... a rock?"

It was only an expensive gemstone inlaid into an opulent broach. "Useless!"

"Worse than useless," muttered the donkey who shook free a pair of stubby spider wings on its dusty back.

"What's that you say, Sassafras?"

Heehaw! was his only irksome reply.

"Still, we have a gentleman in our possession. A lord, it seems." She examined the unconscious noble.

"A shame to waste a tongue lashing," rejoined Sassafras. The tincture was indeed potent, but the ingredients were costly to procure.

She thought a moment. She had waited eagerly to snare a pompous prince. "Perhaps he commands a beautiful property surrounded by fields of golden grain?" She pondered a moment, then banged hard against the backdoor of the pub. The proprietor opened up, demanding to know what the wench wanted.

"What will this fetch me?" she asked, holding up the large gemstone.

"A barrel of our finest mead, madam." He reached for it, and she pulled back. "And a meal for a lady and her, uh, trusty steed there."

"A bed for the week," she added. He nodded in agreement. But she held back.

"Dicker me not," warned the bartender, brandishing his knife.

"And some hay," said Sassafras.

The bewildered barkeep obliged and reached for the glinting object, but again, she hesitated. So, he upped the offer, "I'll throw in a hog's head."

"Sold!" She flung the jewel carelessly at the man. He held the prize close to his heart and then hid it in his apron.

Then his attention turned to the body in the alley. "Did I hear that man there say something about wanting hay? Is he with you?"

"No, my love. You go prepare our supper. I will get rid of the vagabond." He nodded in compliance and exited the alley.

The old woman stood over her fallen prey. She uttered a swirl of damning utterances too profane for this text. The air around her turned black as the wind drew power from her corrupted aura.

Her favorite finger stretched forth and burst into flame. She made a slicing motion with her hand, and Marvyn's body was split open down the center, revealing his heart, lungs, and other succulent organs, still twitching in normal operation. Despite the unholy incision, the patient remained unphased.

"Oh, decisions, decisions," she said, examining the buffet before her.

Sassafras flapped his wings anxiously. "The lungs, you bitter old witch!"

She clasped her chest gently. "Yes, these ancient lungs of mine are a bit worse for wear." Her voice was suddenly frail.

The donkey brayed. "Suits you right. Smoking all them bog bodies."

The old woman chortled, for these were indeed pleasurable moments of sulfuric ecstasy, "How else could I capture their essence, huh?"

"Have you tried a net?" retorted the donkey.

"Hush up, Sassy; I need to concentrate." She licked her parched, wrinkled lips as she prepared mentally and physically, and emotionally to perform the ritual ancient. To distillate the forces of the unknowable into the physical realm was a task requiring single-minded resolve.

She raised both arms high into the air and then spoke in the same vulgar tongue as before and ushered the spirits from within to devour the remnants of her unsavory soul. In return, they plunged into her decrepit form and pulled her blackened lungs from her aching bosom. Another scaly limb eternal snatched the aristocratic lungs from the young physique and the two were swapped.

A ball of light materialized, encompassing the alley. And then it evaporated into the obscured dimness of nothing. A twinge of lifeforce entered them both.

The old witch rose to her feet. *I have the lungs of a young, well-fed lordling.* She breathed in, then exhaled, coughing up putrid blood. *Must be an after-effect of the transformation.* She decided to keep the man alive in case she needed her old lungs returned.

She closed him up like a wardrobe and he woke.

"My head!" he moaned, sitting up. "I must have fainted from the intensity of my first kiss."

"Sir, are you well?" asked the witch.

"I, uh, yes. I must go. I need to sell my grandmother's broach. I must hire the doctor."

"The doctor?" asked the witch.

"Yes, I am very sick. My mother recently passed from the red influenza. And now I have fallen under its grip. I really must get to the market with my..." he searched his person for the broach. "I must have dropped it. Oh, the maiden! She must know where it fell."

His eyes widened as if a spell had been lifted. "That devious little tart!" She had beguiled him somehow, leading him astray down the path of the wicked. "Though, I feel now as though my lungs, while feeble, have been revived of the illness."

"You have the red what, pray tell?" The witch tried to stand and summon the dark spirits once more. But she was too weak.

He answered smiling, "They say once it claims your lungs you can never recover."

Marvyn thought about the missing maiden. *Was she a demon temptress, or rather an angel; had her kiss actually saved me from certain death?*

"That maiden was right about one thing. It is a day of miracles!" And with that, he tore off back the way he came.

Aspect of Hunger

Jesse Chen

I flung another fistful of dirt at the diced-up corpse, shivering as the midnight chill blew straight through my tattered dress. Rocky soil dug into my bare knees. My eyes tracked the rivulets of dark crimson soaking into the ditch, bleeding out the aspect—or innate magical power—of overlord Marek's latest victim. I needed that power.

And I needed Overseer Brandt to leave soon. The pain gnawing on my insides demanded it.

Soon, I promised my hunger. *Soon*.

"Faster, underborn," Brandt spat. "I don't got all night."

My arm wrapped around my bony ribs, begging them to stop aching for a second so I could think straight. He never stayed this long.

"Overseer," I groveled, "I c-can finish burying the traitor. Do not let my weakness keep you from a w-warm bed and wine."

His eyes narrowed under the light of the full moon. My heart skipped a beat—maybe this was the end. Brandt would turn me to ash with his fire aspect for daring to give him a suggestion, and no one would be left to avenge Jacob. So unfair that some people were born with unique abilities that let them create fire or manipulate metal or read minds, while an aspectless like me couldn't do anything but squirm like worms in the dirt.

But my fears didn't materialize. With a *hrmph*, he stalked off. "Pathetic woman. If ya slack off during the mornin' shift, I'll beat ya twice as hard!"

The moment his figure vanished over the ridge, I leaped for the corpse. My fingers tore into the gashes inflicted by Marek's wind aspect. I'd seen him in action before. With a flick of his hand, he could call forth blades of concentrated air that targeted vitals with deadly precision. This poor soul died fast.

Marek must've been in a good mood tonight.

Forcing open the chest cavity was never hard; the overlord always dealt the final blow straight through the heart. It was his signature—a smile of red ripped straight through the left ribs and exited the back. He hadn't even spared Jacob from that, but Jacob's small chest split completely off. No smiling.

I lowered my head, grimy hair dragging against the soil, and sank my teeth into the cooling heart.

No, whimpered my remaining humanity.

Yes, moaned my hunger.

Molten power flowed into my belly. Unbidden, tiny gouts of flame flickered across my knuckles, catching my eye as I feasted. When there was nothing left of the heart but the blood dripping down my chin, I slipped back and fell on my butt, hugging my knees to my chest as tears tracked clean lines down my dirt-streaked face.

How much longer? How much longer would I have to keep doing this?

I concentrated on the burning sensation in my veins as clouds drowned out the moon. A tongue of flame flashed from my palm, hovering like werelight. This was the first flame aspect I'd consumed, and what a weak one it was. I often wished that someone with a poison aspect would look at Marek the wrong way so I could steal their powers and end this. But poison was rare, and overlord Marek's cruelty was surpassed only by his paranoia.

A stumble, a stagger, and I was back on my feet on the path back to the keep, dragging one of the cracked ribs along with me. *Rare.* I'd known a thing or two about that. I was born aspectless, after all, and I'd never heard of anyone with my strange ability.

The memory of tasting my first aspect still haunted me. Marek's son, Sylas, took great pleasure in humiliating all the underborns, and I was his favorite target. One day, Overseer Brandt hauled me away from tilling the field and into the keep, where Sylas presented me with a human heart cut into slices. Maybe from an underborn who stepped out of line.

"I have a present for you," he giggled. "Eat it, underborn."

"Please, m-my lord, I am not worthy," I said, flinching away from the smell of death.

His expression switched like a snuffed-out candle. "I'm the boss, which means you'll eat whatever I tell you to eat!"

I glanced at Overseer Brandt, but there'd been no mercy there. I suppressed a gag and choked down the chewy flesh that burned all the way into my stomach. Half of it came out with bile. I received the whipping of my life and had to clean it up after.

But the other half stayed down, and my veins writhed like a thousand insects. The world spun out of control as I staggered back to my straw cot. My two-year-old, Jacob, cried for milk that I didn't have. Fuzzy voices murmured above, and when the ceiling finally stopped chasing the floor, I stumbled up. It was so bright. I thought I'd missed my shift.

The field was deserted, and the torches were lit. And the moon! *The moon is out in the middle of the day!* It took me a long time to figure out that I'd actually woken up at night, and instead I could see as if it were noon. Somehow, I'd gained an aspect.

Sylas' "present" was the first aspect I'd consumed. I named it *Owl*.

Owl lit up my world now, tearing away the veil of night. Judging from the brightness, I had a few minutes to make it home before my aspect failed. It was drawing on energy that didn't exist in my flagging limbs. I needed to hurry. The keep loomed above me, and I snuck in through the servant's entrance.

"Come on, Cat, don't fail me now," I muttered, hoping that the feline aspect would sharpen my senses. I smelled the beer on a sleepy guard's breath, felt every groove in the ground as I tiptoed past. Every noise, from creaking wood and quiet exhalations, told me the positions of sentries and the best path to evade them. There was no sense in taking risks or drawing attention to myself, especially with my mouth covered in blood.

Thank goodness Marek hadn't liked his first wife. Cat helped make this all possible.

A low growl greeted me as I inched closer to the keep's center. I needed to pass Seth, the guard dog, if I wanted to reach my hut by the stables. He stalked toward me with massive paws as large as my head. Drool dripped from sharp fangs that I'd seen bring down a full-grown stag. I raised my forearm defensively, calling forth the aspect I regretted the most. I had named it *Armor*.

Seth's jaw clamped over skin that hardened like tempered steel. I couldn't feel a thing. Whenever I came back from burying Marek's latest kill, we engaged in this little ritual. The first time, he thought I was an intruder. After that, I think he was just lonely.

"Good boy," I whispered, teasing him with the cracked rib. He snapped at it happily, releasing my forearm and allowing me to sneak back to my flimsy abode.

Owl flickered and ran out, drowning the world in darkness as I lay down on the pile of straw that served as my bed. A sliver of moonlight remained, illuminating my wispy breath as I pulled out my son's patchwork doll from underneath my burlap sack pillow.

"I'm almost strong enough, Jacob," I told it. "If I just keep eating, someday I'll be more powerful than Marek. Fire aspects, plant aspects, bring them all on."

The button eyes stared back at me.

"I'll make sure you didn't die for nothing."

I lay back onto the straw and clutched the doll against my chest.

"I'm worried, Jacob. I'm too weak."

But the doll stayed silent, and soon my fatigued mind drifted off to dreams of sticking a sharp knife down Marek's throat.

I woke up to Overseer Brandt dragging me off my cot. I knew better than to resist. He tossed my limp frame like a sack of potatoes onto the street, where a pointed boot tapped a menacing beat on the cobblestones.

"Good morning, underborn," Marek sneered. "Sir Brandt tells me you ate a human heart. Are you sick in the head?"

My stomach lurched. I kept my head against the dirt, not daring to look up. *How had they known?* "N-no, over-lord. I would never—"

"She lies," Brandt said. "She was takin' too long with the bodies, so I went out this morning to see. It weren't even buried!"

I'd forgotten to cover the body last night! How could I have been so careless?

"Please f-forgive your worthless underborn. I was... I was hungry."

So hungry, growled the beast in my belly. I could smell the power in their veins, pulsating, so close that all I had to do was lunge and...

No! I bit my tongue, locking my muscles in place.

Marek laughed. "Only to be expected. But I can't have people spreading rumors about what I do here. No more burial duty for you, I'm afraid. Oh, but where are my manners—you haven't eaten breakfast yet. Here, there's some dirt on the underside of my boot that I suppose you may have."

I peeked at the dirt-caked leather in front of my face. "Please, l-lord, I—*ah!*"

Pain lanced up my side as Brandt kicked me. "How dare ya turn down the lord's generosity? Ya said 'hungry;' get to it!"

Their jeers rang loud in my ears as I dragged my tongue across the filth.

Afterward, I still needed to join the others in the field. My stomach gurgled. Dirt and emptiness rumbled around inside as I stumbled through the even rows, picking wheat that I would never eat, smelling the rich soil all around me.

What am I supposed to do now?

Without aspects to consume, how was I supposed to become strong enough to avenge Jacob?

There, in the field of gold, tasting grit on my tongue, something broke. A dam, a wall, something deep within that had been sheltering my despair. It all cracked, and the overwhelming fear poured in.

I am going to die here.

I was going to die, and Jacob's life was nothing more than a fly that a nobleman swatted. Nothing more than a pest in the past.

No, I wouldn't let that happen. Couldn't let that happen.

That night, I drew upon Owl and Cat to sneak into the darkened keep. A jagged rock dug into the palm of my hand—a rock meant for Marek's throat. It had served here before when his cleaning underborns fell sick, and with every step I took closer to his room, the rumbling inside grew in waves upon waves.

I was not prepared to see Overseer Brandt sitting in front of the great oak doors, snores rumbling from his oafish mouth. I did not think Marek was so paranoid that he would make the overseer stand guard. If it were anyone else, I might be able to overpower them, but Brandt was too strong for me.

Is he?

I crept closer, rock shaking as I raised it toward Brandt's jugular. The blood howled in his veins, in my ears. I plunged the rock into his pale flesh.

A crimson fountain erupted. *Too shallow!* His eyes shot open. Brandt roared awake, his meaty fist ripping my hand away from his throat as he slapped a palm over the wound to stanch the bleeding.

I kicked and struggled as he dragged me down the hall, but neither of us made much sound. He didn't want to wake Marek. I didn't want him to raise the alarm. The world spun as he hurled me into the far wall of an empty room with a sickening crack. The air rushed from my lungs.

Move, I begged my muscles. *Please!*

Feast, screamed the beast in my belly.

"You got a lotta nerve," Brandt sneered as he closed the door, hand still pressed to his neck. Searing pain consumed my ribcage as a ball of flame exploded against my side. A howl erupted from my throat. I rolled to the side, narrowly dodging a second burst of fire.

Cat boiled to the surface, letting me jump to the side as I called on my Flame aspect. It was so weak compared to Brandt's. The overseer laughed at my pitiful embers before bathing the room in fire.

Air. Not enough air! My knee hit the ground with a crunch as black smoke billowed around my head. Brandt loomed over me. I saw his boot move before my head smashed into something and the world went blurry. Dark spots flickered in my vision. Owl was collapsing; so was Cat.

Brandt's steel-grip clenched around my throat, forcing my body up. I swatted at him feebly, but he didn't even bother dodging. As my vision faded to stars, I felt wetness on my cheek.

Blood. Brandt's blood.

With the remaining strength in my body, I licked at the crimson rivulets running down my cheek.

Yes, sighed the monster in my belly. *Yes.*

Power shook my limbs as my body went red hot. Brandt yelped and let go, but my muscles moved on their own. My teeth sank into his finger. A crunch, another yell, and blood dribbled onto my tongue. I met his next fireball with one of my own.

Mine was bigger.

I jumped onto his shoulders with a strength I didn't know I had. Blood. Fresh blood, that was the difference.

My dirty nails tore at his wound, pawing and sucking at the dripping cut on his neck as he tried to shake me off. Flames exploded around me in an unholy wreath that dyed my vision orange. Slowly, his flailing limbs and panicked gasps weakened, then faded into stillness.

More, crooned my stomach. I drank until the world sharpened and I could breathe again.

Steel-tipped boots pounded on the stone hallway floor. Soldiers burst into the room, shouting words that fell on deaf ears as the jet of flame bursting from my arm hurled them out.

Their screams stopped. My fire didn't.

My soot-stained feet padded over their smoking corpses as my fingers pried into them for their powers. It wasn't enough. *Not nearly enough!* Marek was more powerful than Brandt, so I guzzled the bright red wine of their life until my stomach felt like bursting. I knew these guards had Strength. They would come in handy.

But there was no time to play around. The object of my hatred lay up ahead, so I formed two concentrated balls of fire and sent them through the door. Everything would burn.

Two slashes of wind answered, but I used all the energy in my gut to power my Armor aspect. The air dissipated against me without a scratch, and I was stunned in disbelief.

He couldn't stop me.

I charged into the room, rushing toward overlord Marek as he channeled a tornado. His wind collided with the flames billowing out from my limbs, and the inferno greedily sucked in air. The energy that Marek funneled into his creation exploded, sending both of us flying. The back of my head smacked against the stone wall, and I fell to my knees, vision swimming.

By the time I stumbled to my feet, Marek had already prepared swirling gusts of wind that launched objects at me: dressers, chairs, shards of glass and stone. I countered these with my new strength aspect, but the energy in my gut was fading fast.

I was running out of time.

He ran out of things to throw at me and sent a barrage of wind blades flying my way. I hardened my skin, but Armor weakened with every slash. With the last dregs of energy in my body and Jacob on my mind, I charged forward and tackled Marek to the ground.

We struggled and rolled, a tangle of limbs, before coming to a rest at the foot of his bed. He lashed out with blades of wind that had never failed to cut people into ribbons before. They broke against me.

I broke his limbs one by one. When he stopped screaming, I sat on his chest. My hands clenched around his throat.

"Why can't I cut you? You're aspectless!"

I relished the way his eyes jittered as he looked for a way out. "The gift of one of your victims. It's my Armor."

"No! I would have remembered an underborn with that aspect!"

A croaking laugh scratched at my ears, and I realized it was my own. "You wouldn't remember him. He was only a child. His name was Jacob."

I remembered the tiny broken body, the vacant eyes, the tears streaming down my face.

I remembered eating his malnourished heart.

Marek's eyes widened, but I couldn't wait a moment longer. I tightened my grip and let the beast in my belly roar as loud as it pleased.

White flames of rage erupted from my hands. Marek screamed and struggled, but I held on as tongues of fire licked at his clothes, his hair, devoured his eyes, and finally silenced him forever.

I sat there, warm in the midst of ashes, before the heat became too much.

After freeing the rest of the underborns, I fled the keep as it went up in flames. Dark red light lit up the night clouds. I knew not where I was going, only that it was no longer painful to walk.

My hunger was quiet at last.

Joust Between Friends

Allison Tebo

To anyone who knew her, it was no secret that Salome had a soft spot for hard-luck cases.

Salome might attract the attention of the local sheriffs and their men in every town she traveled through, but she left a string of good deeds behind her that more than made up for the trouble she carried with her.

Today was no different. On a sunny market day in the little town of Chetwold, Salome saw someone in need and tried to help. The fact that he might also be a sound business investment was merely honey on the porridge.

She found her next champion standing at the edge of the crowded square.

She headed casually in his direction, pausing briefly by a booth selling new spell lamps—magic vessels of floating illumination. They made life easier for those who could afford them, but only people working in government were allowed to purchase any product involving magic.

Salome checked the price on the wooden plaque and snorted. She sold them for half that price, and her customers didn't need government papers. Additionally, hers came in four different colors.

"I'm a hero," she muttered, moving away from the stall and heading toward the stranger, circling around him for a better look. He was definitely a lusty fellow. Undoubtedly, he would have a lot of power behind that arm.

He was selling his horse to a royal official; the only citizens who had extra coin these days. It was a fine-looking horse, a stallion with strong hindquarters and heavy bones: the kind of beast usually owned by a knight. Salome suspected that the man was a former crusader. And, like most veteran crusaders, he looked as though he had gone a round or two with some bad fortune. His clothes had once been fine but were now worn and dirty.

There was something especially sad about a warrior without something to fight. It was like rust on a forgotten sword: a shame and a waste.

Besides, her current champion's glory days were fading. Ablehard the Awful had served her well, winning them both considerable profits in wagers. But since he was now proving to be better at lifting a tankard than his lance, it was time to find a new champion.

She made her decision and approached.

"Good morning," she said, tipping her head to the man. "That's a fine horse. 'Tis a pity you had to sell it."

"Aye," the man agreed, bowing and studying her with narrow eyes. "That it is."

"If I were to make my guess, that was a charger's mount, and you fought in the foreign wars." She elbowed him in the ribs. "Am I right?"

The man nodded.

Salome smiled. "I suspected as much. What's your name, friend, and what's your story?"

"William Berringer. I fought as a freeman under Sir James the Lionheart."

"Let me hazard another guess. When the war ended, you returned home only to find that there was no place for you in your line of work. You spent nearly everything you owned for the journey back, and now you are selling your sword and horse so you can get by until you find employment."

William's eyebrows shot up, but he nodded again. "I suppose there are many men with the same story these days." Salome clucked her tongue in sympathy. "Well, friend Berringer, today fortune smiles upon you. It just so happens that I need a warrior."

William cocked his head. "You are in need of protection?"

Salome twiddled with the folds of her dress. "Oh no, nothing of that nature. I am in need of, what you might call…a champion." Salome laced her arm through his. "Come with me, and I'll tell you all about my proposition. Er, by the by, how are you at holding your liquor?"

William shrugged. "It's easy enough to hold it when you never take much."

Salome patted his arm. "I knew I liked you from the moment I saw you."

* * *

Salome bought back William's horse for him and they set off together.

By the time they reached the nearby forest, Salome had made it clear that her line of work wasn't strictly legal.

William, however, bore the news stoically and with little surprise. He assured her he was willing to do anything.

Salome batted a tree branch out of her way and turned in her saddle. "Young man, with that kind of determination, you'll go far in life. And now I'm afraid I'll have to blindfold you." She waited a minute, giving him a chance to back out, but William didn't flinch. She smiled, pleased. "The way to success," she said as she tied the blindfold around his eyes, "is to know your market. And, after careful study, it has become clear to me that the most secure trade in the world is anything illegal. There is something about human nature that makes the forbidden utterly irresistible and worth any price."

William chuckled. "It has always seemed to me that most people like rules—they make people feel safe."

"Yes, well, I try not to associate with people of that ilk."

William saw nothing of the next three miles; not the circuitous route, the hidden clearing, or the hidden cave entrance—one of many entrances into the den of iniquity.

Salome lit a torch and took William by the hand, leading him past the cover of undergrowth and into the darkness of the cave.

"It's nothing personal, you understand," she explained. "Just a precaution, due to the unyielding nature of the local law enforcement."

William cleared his throat. "What, exactly, makes this illegal, if I might ask?"

"Oh, just a little crowd-pleasing violence. No one's ever hurt. Well," she amended with a cough, "there have been a few lads that were maimed, but those things happen."

"Life's hard," William agreed.

"Exactly my way of thinking! For the most part, I've never seen so many happy men. Why, just the other day, I heard a man say his girl had been so impressed by seeing him bash another fellow that she accepted his proposal." She pulled William down yet another winding tunnel. "I think you'll find this work just as fulfilling as I do. It's better than selling potions."

William's mouth twisted as if he was going to laugh, though Salome wasn't sure why. "What made you quit the potion trade?"

"The market dried up," Salome sighed. Yes, it was a good line of work she had found. Though, her previous scheme had been satisfying too, in its own way. Salome had long held the belief that most of the ailing people of the world were actually suffering from imagined maladies, and they could be cured easily if they simply believed they were better.

As it turned out, Salome was right. Nearly half the population felt better after drinking blueberry juice. It wasn't really her fault that it didn't work for the other half. At least she—unlike other potion makers—was giving them a product that tasted good.

All had gone more-or-less well until the day Salome stumbled across a little boy crying from hunger. Salome had given him a bag of potions to sell so that he could eat. When the boy had asked what they were, Salome thoughtlessly replied that they didn't really do anything, they just tasted nice.

Unfortunately, the laundress eavesdropping on them didn't appreciate her honesty.

Salome had been firmly encouraged to leave that town by a rambunctious crowd. She liked to believe that they were such a generous people, they couldn't stand to keep her all to themselves. It was only because they didn't have any flowers on hand that they had been reduced to throwing rocks and vegetables.

Salome ducked around a pile of boulders, pulling William along by the hand and occasionally warning him of low-hanging stalactites and the puddles beneath around them, but William was surprisingly sure-footed for being blindfolded.

A few times, she noticed that William appeared to be sniffing at the air. Frowning, she gave an experimental sniff of her own. It hadn't occurred to her that the smell of dead bats might be unappealing for her customers; she had always assumed that the aroma of pipe tobacco and ale drowned it out. She made a quick mental note to purchase sweet-smelling herbs and incense in town.

Salome did a little jig of excitement as they stepped into the main chamber, and she whipped the blindfold from William's eyes. "Behold!"

William's eyes bulged.

"An... illegal jousting den?"

Salome flung an arm around his frozen shoulders. "Isn't it marvelous?"

* * *

Ever since the last crusade when over half of the country's men had been killed in foreign wars, jousting had been outlawed.

Salome didn't think that law was quite fair. Sure their population had dwindled, making labor hard to find, but if a man felt the desperate need to prove his strength and skill by taking a lance to the gut, who was she to stop him?

Unfortunately, due to some knavish law, if anyone involved with Salome's business was caught they would be thrown into prison, with regular visits to the public stocks for some character-forming humiliation. It was more than likely that Salome herself would probably be hung.

It had bothered her at first, to think that there were people in this world so prudish that they couldn't tolerate a little harmless entertainment and bloodshed. Still, based on the success of her venture, it was clear that there were still many people willing to bend the rules.

People like William, apparently. There was nothing but admiration on his face as he looked around.

"Welcome to Salome's Jousting of the Underworld!" Salome waved a hand grandly at their surroundings.

They were standing in an immense cavern with a flat, sandy floor. The cave was lit by dozens of colored spell vessels, casting a brilliant illumination far brighter than candles and causing the chamber to be brighter than any other establishment in Chetwold. The cavern was roughly a hundred yards long and fifty wide, more than enough room for the list—the runway used for the jousting match. The runway was designated by ropes stretched between stalagmites. Outside the ropes, chairs, and tables had been set up for attendees to get a good look at the action.

In one corner, a kind of tavern had been set up with a low wooden plank set across barrels to serve as a bar. Shelves of tankards sat behind, ready to serve thirsty guests.

Along one end of the cavern, there was an opening in the stone wall where a low chamber curved around in a half-circle. It was the perfect place for the highest-paying tradesmen to set up shop.

Salome pointed to it. "Tradespeople can sell their own goods there, as long as they pay a small fee to me for the privilege." She rubbed her hands together. "I'm expecting fortune tellers and all manner of bakers here tonight."

William turned in a slow circle. "This is incredible."

Salome bowed deeply. "Thank you, thank you. I know it is."

William rubbed his beard. "An illegal jousting ring and a tax-free market."

Salome nodded. "Do you know how much tax these poor people would be forced to pay if it weren't for me? Fifty percent! They can barely subsist as it is," she said, "and the lawmen call me a criminal. Nay, I provide a service! Peasants have a chance to keep some of their hard-earned coin and pathetic, broken warriors—such as yourself—have an opportunity to make a living at what they do best. And for this, I am willing to risk my life."

Salome sighed as she paused to consider her own largesse. "So, here's my proposition, friend. I've got four men I'm considering to replace my retiring champion. I like the look of you, Berringer. I think you have what it takes to win. Do you?"

Berringer gave her a thin smile. "I do hate to lose."

"I could tell," Salome said approvingly. "You have the horse. We'll provide the lance and armor. If you're good enough, you will be the last man standing in the arena."

William eyed the lists. "I'm good enough."

"I like a man with confidence!" She patted him on the shoulder. "Yes, indeed, everything's going to work out just fine. But first, I have to discharge Awful."

She moved to the tavern corner, weaving her way through the handful of workers scattered about the cavern who were preparing for tonight's festivities. William followed her curiously.

Ablehard the Awful was face-down on one of the tavern's makeshift tables. Salome grabbed a handful of his bushy hair and pulled him upright. "Greetings, Awful! I'm sorry to inform you, but you won't be jousting for me anymore."

Ablehard jerked away from her, flapping and gasping like a fish drawn out of water. "Wha-what? You can't do that to me! I'm your—*hic*—champion!"

Were, Salome silently amended, regarding him with pity. "You can still work for me." She could keep him on to lug barrels. "But it's better to rest on your laurels as a champion of the underworld than to take a tumble and lose the people's praise, don't you agree?"

Ablehard furrowed his brow as if in pain. "I suppose."

She put an arm around his shoulder. "You don't want people to know that you're a failure, do you?" She swayed suddenly and gripped her stomach. "Ablehard, all of this arguing is giving me great pain!"

Ablehard's scowl crumpled into a look of guilt. "I'm sorry, Salome. Whatever you say. I'll quit!"

Salome patted him weakly. "Thank you." Still clutching her stomach, she tottered toward the tavern bar, where Philip, one of her assistants, polished a lance.

With one last bemused look at Ablehard, William followed her. "Are you all right?"

"I've had terrible pains in the gut for years." Salome held out her hand to Phillip, who reached beneath the bar and slipped a flask into her hand. "When you're a public benefactor, it takes a toll on you." She took a swig from the flask and sighed. "But this stomach elixir keeps me alive."

She caught Phillip's eye and let her mouth twitch to acknowledge his wink. All her men knew that the elixirs were berry juice and that her gut was healthy. But sometimes, when disputes broke out, it was useful to have a pity-play up your sleeve.

William pointed to the color spell lights lining the edges of the cave.

Salome tugged one toward her and polished the crystalline surface with a sleeve.

"Pretty, aren't they? I get them in bulk from an old crone I know. Fairly soon, every wife will want one, and every man will be buying one for his sweetheart. As long as they're kept hidden from the lawmen, that is."

The ale was flowing, the cheers were rising and, best of all, the coins were clinking in the coffers.

"Isn't it wonderful?" Salome bellowed in William's ear, clapping with the rest of the crowd. "See how everyone's enjoying themselves? How could we deprive them of their entertainment during such troubled times?"

"Indeed!" William called back.

Salome looked around at the festive scene. A nasty cave that smelled of dead bats had been turned into an enchanted fair.

The guests had been a little put out to hear that Ablehard had been retired without a final victory round. Salome gave them all a free round of ale and they stopped grumbling, drinking a toast to the former underworld champion, much to Ablehard's delight. Salome reflected that it was times like these that made the risks all worthwhile.

Salome leaned against the ropes and watched as the contestants tilted at one another for a third and final time. The hooves of their galloping horses filled the cavern with thunder that was nearly lost in the roar of the crowd as the blue knight was knocked off his horse by a blow to the kneecap.

Unlike the often-dull legal matches that had been seen in the past, Salome had upped the excitement. Blows could be given to any place an attacker wished, albeit with one stipulation: matches were officially over as soon as a knight was dismounted. After an unfortunate incident where a pair of knights destroyed the tavern and the livelihood of an apple monger, Salome had decided that matches could not be continued on the ground.

Salome took a swig from her tankard. Tonight, after watching her four candidates perform, she would be selecting a new house champion. She felt supremely confident that William would be her man. There was something reassuring about him.

He looked like the kind of oaf that would rather die than fail. That type of man was always a safe bet.

There was a brief lull in the festivities as Salome was called upon to decide whether throwing your lance like a spear was allowed.

When she returned to her place in the audience, she found that William was gone.

Salome growled in irritation. She had wanted William to watch the matches to get an idea of what sort of operation she was hosting. She hurried through the roaring crowds, searching for her would-be-champion. It was nearly time for William to fight; where was he?

A commotion at the cavern's main entrance caught her attention. Salome sucked in her breath as screams erupted throughout the arena, echoing throughout the cave and grew into a roar.

Men wearing the sheriff's infamous yellow and green poured into the cavern.

The knights still mounted, left off bashing one another with maces and sent their mounts breaking through the ropes as they raced towards the back exit to escape, leaving a trail of fresh chaos in their wake.

The lawmen's sudden rush checked as the crowd turned to defend themselves, throwing whatever came to hand: food, tankards, or team pennants.

Salome, who had been knocked down when a cowardly knight and his screaming horse stampeded past her, crawled to her feet, then ducked again as an arrow whizzed past her ear. "Surrender peacefully!" Salome bellowed. She didn't want anybody getting killed.

A boot from one of the sheriff's men went flying over her head, followed immediately by a badly-torn jerkin and a hat. No one was listening to her.

"Run for it, Salome!" Phillip bellowed as the rest of Salome's men closed rank in front of her.

Salome raced by them, blowing kisses, overwhelmed by their generosity. If only her business had still been in operation, she would have given them a bonus.

She tore into the shadows on the left, heading for a narrow tunnel used exclusively by her and her employees.

The hilt of a sword was suddenly thrust out ahead of her from behind a boulder.

Salome, unaccustomed to running, was also unaccustomed to stopping in a hurry. Her stomach did the job for her by slamming into the sword's pommel.

She looked up from her prone position on the ground and squinted at the figure standing over her.

It was William.

"What?" Salome gasped, clutching at her stomach and gaping up at him. "You?"

"Me," William said grimly. "Come on, let's go,"

Since Salome was incapable of walking after William's little surprise, she was dragged unceremoniously into the clearing where she had brought William that same morning and thrown on the ground beside thirty others who had been arrested, including Phillip and Ablehard.

Most of the guests and competing knights had escaped the sheriff's clutches. But that was small comfort to Salome, who was still nursing her stomach, as well as a sense of betrayal.

She glowered afresh as a guard produced rope to tie her hands and ankles.

"Oh for pity's sake!" Salome snorted. "As if I could do anything after the blow that traitor gave me? And besides, do I look like a runner to you?"

The guard eyed her well-rounded frame. "In all honesty, no."

Salome was not insulted. She would have gone even further to convince him, too, if it meant she remained untied.

Perhaps William felt guilty for nearly killing her with his pommel because he motioned for the guard to let her alone.

Salome was left to writhe on the ground and reflect on the unfairness of life. It seemed this was always the way of things. The moment she started being kind to someone, fate spat in her eye.

She watched glumly as lawmen funneled out of the tunnels, making piles of her goods and hard-earned coin.

The sheriff, a thoroughly disagreeable-looking man with a pock-marked face and unkempt hair, stomped over to Salome.

"Let that be a lesson to tax avoiders. You didn't think you could hide from us forever, did you?"

The sheriff smirked at her obvious discomfort. "Berringer served us well in the foreign wars, but now his unusual talents have proved that he is even more useful here.

"I can't believe I bought your horse back for you," Salome said to William. She wanted to smash her face against a rock, but she ached enough as it was.

William crouched and met her judgmental gaze.

"So... you lied to me," she said.

"You've already said that ten times," William remarked, unruffled.

Salome wriggled impatiently. "And? Don't you have something to say? Don't you feel the least bit sorry about doing this to me?"

"It's my job."

"Well your job is terrible," Salome said coldly. "And, I'm sorry to say it, but you must have a brain the size of a walnut. You passed over a chance to make some real gold in favor of these jesters." She studied him. "When you were sniffing in the cave, you were using your magic to make a map of sorts, weren't you?"

Salome detected the tell-tale twitch of confirmation in his face. She whistled, annoyance temporarily forgotten. "How does that even work?"

"That's no concern of yours," William responded shortly.

Salome's mind spun with possibilities. A man who could see even while blindfolded! She let herself imagine fortune-telling acts, divination displays, perhaps even a little innocent blackmailing.

She edged closer to William. "Help me escape. I'll forgive you, and we'll go into business together. We could do great things."

William's mouth twitched. "I like my job."

Salome goggled at him. "Working for the government?" Clearly, they were not destined to be friends after all.

A deputy emerged out of the tunnel and whispered in the sheriff's ear.

The sheriff rounded on Salome. "Where are your coffers, thief? My men can't find anything but tonight's profits."

Salome sniffed. She might be generous to a fault, and her friendliness might be her blind spot, but she still had some fundamental intelligence. Only a fool would keep her coffers in plain sight.

She gestured bitterly to William. "Why don't you use your magic hunting dog to locate them?"

The sheriff raised a hand to strike her, but William spoke up, "Let me speak with her."

The sheriff looked between them and then moved away, scowling.

William leaned over Salome. "Cooperate, and the sheriff might be convinced to treat you more easily."

Salome gave William a pitying look. The poor man actually believed such nonsense.

Struck with a new idea, she doubled up and rubbed her belly. "Oh, my stomach!" she shouted. "I'm dying!"

The sheriff snorted, "If you think you're dying now, just wait till we finish questioning you."

Salome pointed an accusing finger at William. "He hit me in the stomach. The least you could do is show a little mercy." She groaned again. "If I die now you'll never be able to question me," she warned. "Just let me take some of my stomach elixir, please!"

The sheriff raised an eyebrow and glanced at William, who nodded in confirmation. "It's true. She does have a wasting disease."

The sheriff grimaced. "Fine. Take your elixir."

Salome removed a vial from her pocket and gave it a good shake. The sheriff's men stepped closer, drawing their bowstrings taut.

She raised a hand. "No need to get excited. Just one swig of this and everything will be alright."

She brought the vial to her lips.

William started. "That's not the same bottle you were drinking from earlier—"

Salome swallowed quickly... and disappeared.

* * *

For a moment, the clearing was utterly silent.

"Well, I'll be," Phillip murmured. "Those magic potions of hers actually work after all!"

At his words, pandemonium broke out.

All of the captured men and women immediately began wriggling about to try and wrest potions from hiding places that the sheriff's men had overlooked. They toppled onto their sides or doubled over in an attempt to pull the corks from their respective bottles with their teeth. Ablehard was so anxious to disappear that he put the entire bottle in his mouth in an attempt to swallow it.

Flopping over without warning caused them to trip members of the sheriff's party who were racing about, searching for Salome. The few lawmen still standing, pounced on the confiscated potions box and began ripping through it as the sheriff yelled at them to cease plundering the king's property.

William stood in the center of it all, completely bewildered.

Standing a hundred feet away, still unseen to human eyes, Salome chuckled as she watched the mad scramble. *Poor children. They would be disappointed. But at least whatever useless potion they drank would be tasty. Let it never be said that Salome cheated a customer.*

A Silent Vengeance

Zoë Freeman

Theron moved through the halls of his father's keep. The vaulted stone corridors carried the echoes of his footsteps, and the air hummed with the guttering of torch fire, but all else was silent. Though the hour was deep in the night, he was fully dressed and walked with purpose through the dim pools of light. This purpose had been driving him for too long. He'd have come to it sooner, but greater plans were at risk. Tonight, though, his wait was over.

The path he took was as familiar to him as the rhythm of his own breathing. He had walked these halls for the length of his life and could have found the way blindfolded. Twenty-nine years in the same rows of stone, cast in the same shadows. In his youth, he had cowered from such shadows, then he'd sought refuge in them. Eventually, he'd learned to thrive, bide his time and build his power from within them, but the time had finally come to part with them.

Twenty-nine years—a shamefully long time for a man to be a prince. Of course, it had all been necessary. A viper did not show his head until he was ready to strike.

There was more light as he came to the halls that housed the king. Knives could not strike where there was light, or so the king believed. The walls here were lined with elaborate iron sconces that cast an even glow through the corridor, strengthened by the light of wide, burning cauldrons. Theron strode forward, not hesitating even as he was spotted by the squad of four guards posted outside the first set of great wooden doors.

They recognized him at once. He watched the men's grips grow tight on their spears as he approached, their stances stiffening and their expressions uncertain as he crossed the space toward them. They looked to each other for guidance only to find their comrades equally anxious. It wasn't until Theron had nearly reached them that one man came to his senses. He clacked his heels together, straightened his back, and shouldered his weapon in a respectful bow.

"Highness," he said. The others hastily followed his lead. Their unison was disrupted, but by the time Theron stood in their midst, all four pairs of eyes were respectfully fixed on the ground. They parted from his path without resistance and fumbled a disjointed salute at his back as he pushed open the heavy doors with a two-handed shove.

They swung inward, delivering him into a well-lit reception chamber. The guards stationed inside jumped clear of the doors and faced him quickly, leveling their spears. Two more guards jolted alert across the room, standing to block his access to a more ornate set of doors. At first, the men put up their voices in alarm and rushed to draw the short swords at their sides, but their expressions paled when the identity of the intruder settled in. They let their blades slip back into their scabbards with unsteady grips, knocked their heels, and shifted out of his path with their heads bowed.

"Highness," they chorused, though their voices were weak. Theron did nothing to acknowledge them and forced open the doorway they guarded.

A huge hearth was all that illuminated the room beyond; a warm, richly furnished chamber fit for a king. Two final guards waited beside the carved door directly across the fine carpeted floor, and even in the low-glowing light, Theron could see how they wilted at his entrance. Theron advanced toward them, and one man took a swift step aside, standing in a salute. The other man stayed still, however. His hands shook on the shaft of his spear.

Theron stopped before him, wordless. Gaunt, the man swallowed. His brow shone with a thin sheen of sweat, and his breath was unsteady. In his fear, he dared to meet the prince's eyes, but he found them unrelenting. At last, the guard's own eyes grew vacant, and his gaze slipped down to the floor. He shifted to the side, his weapon falling out of the guarding position and into a salute.

"My prince," he said. For all his weakness, his voice was clearer than all the men who'd sworn before him.

Theron narrowed his eyes, then turned his attention back to the door. He heard no movement on the other side, and so he squared his broad shoulders and pushed through the doorway.

He stepped again into shadow and quiet. Another fire was burning beneath an intricate mantle, though the light in this hearth burned low and dim. The shapes of the heavy velvet draperies on the rich poster bed hung like black ghosts, motionless. They were already drawn back and the bedding was empty, but the gleaming silk sheets were rumpled from use.

The king had left his bed in a hurry.

Theron cast his gaze over the dark, but the dancing spears of the fire's light threatened to trick his eyes with false movement. He stood entirely still until at last something stirred to his right, nearly behind him. He looked past his shoulder with deadly speed and raised his defensive arm even faster. His hand caught the shaft of polished wood before it could come down on the back of his head.

He didn't have to look at the object to know exactly what it was. The royal scepter, a dark-wooded staff tipped with metal and topped with the golden Redrian crest. But Theron knew it better like it was now—as a weapon of punishment. In all the years that its owner had brought the scepter down in vengeance, Theron had never raised a hand to stop it.

The shock of the trespass showed in the haggard face of Theron's attacker. King Ambros' cheeks were gaunt. The thick beard of black-and-white peppered whiskers looked like it was pulling the skin of his face down with its weight. His eyes stretched wide beneath a thick, deeply creased brow, upon which rested a circlet of gold that never left its mount there. Disheveled from sleep, he had a wild look about him. Theron curled his lip in distaste before he wrenched the scepter from his father's fingers.

The king staggered back, raising his hands in defense of his person, though as he recognized the face of his intruder, he scowled with anger, not fear.

"You," he said, his lips shaking with ragged breath. "Get out. Leave me at once. Get out of my presence." He cast a finger toward the door, but lost his balance and toppled into a heavy brown table set behind him. The gold and silver wares that covered it toppled in a clamor, and wine spilled from both goblets and pitchers as the king groped to catch his balance. He dropped heavily into a chair and caught one tipping chalice by the neck, and ignored the deep, ruddy color staining the sleeves of his heavy robe as he lifted the cup with a shaking hand to his lips. He drank loudly, but his slurps came to a bubbling stop when he realized that Theron had not moved at his command. He lowered the golden cup, malice burning in his dark eyes.

"Are you deaf now as well, you idiot mute?" he spat. "I told you to get out."

Theron stood still, staring his father down through the flickering gloom. He remained motionless until he could see the king's fists shaking. Ambros' face was going red, even in the dim light. He surged to his feet. "Get out!"

At last, Theron moved, but only to catch the king's arm by the wrist as he flailed it widely to strike at his son.

Old Ambros' whole body jolted when he found his tirade suddenly arrested. He blinked, his arm held extended between him and his son, and in an instant, his face contorted with rage.

"How dare you—" he snarled as he yanked to free himself from Theron's hold. The brocaded silk of his robe helped him slip free but Theron took a handful of the thick fabric and held him in place. He gripped the royal scepter tight before swinging it in a close arc, bringing it down with crushing force into the king's arm.

The moment of shock lasted long enough to hear the sound of bone snapping. The king's eyes shot wide, his mouth gaped open, and then the ragged gasp of pain found its way from his lips.

Theron let his father tear free and stumble back, cradling his broken arm like a child. The king looked up, face a mask of shock and pain. His mouth moved, lips flapping soundlessly, too astonished to speak.

Theron blinked, taking that image into his memory. Then he stepped forward, swinging his father's scepter upright into his palm like a club.

For the first time, Ambros let out a winded scream, but he could not fall back quickly enough before his son bludgeoned the side of his opposite arm with the crested head of the scepter. He toppled to the ground, moaning and trying to grip at his shoulder. His broken arm prevented it, and his hand only shook over the second injury. He held up both hands as Theron stood over him.

"Treason!" he howled, then choked on a groan as Theron brought the scepter savagely down against his soft side. He rolled over, crying out and becoming tangled in his robes. "Murder! Murder to the king!"

Ambros reached out a hand to claw away, but only gasped as Theron ground his heel into his shattered arm. The king gagged, then retched, and might have been sick but for the blow he received in the stomach from Theron's boot. He was thrown onto his back where he wheezed up toward the ceiling. His eyes lolled.

"Murder..." he rasped and struggled to move.

Theron let the scepter hang in his hand, momentarily forgotten. He grimaced down at the pitiful, cowering form of his father, then took a step forward and placed a powerful foot upon the center of the king's chest. A breast that had once been corded and hardened by the vigors of war had grown weak and withered with age, his decline only sped by the vices of idleness and comfort. Theron pressed down on it with the full weight of his own body and felt the air sinking out beneath his boot.

The king writhed and clawed at Theron's leg with the rough, aged fingers of one hand. His eyes rolled in moments of panic, but in the dancing blades of firelight, his wild gaze found his son's face. The helplessness in his expression faded and warped once more into not fear, but rage. His sunken cheeks puffed as he sputtered for air, glaring up from his back.

"You... treacherous... coward... ungrateful..."
Theron pressed harder. The king coughed and groaned heavily, but gritted his teeth and rasped on.

"You won't, not strong enough... won't do it... can't..."
Theron pressed even harder to silence the old fool. He pressed until his father's eyes bulged in his head. The old king floundered. He started pounding Theron's leg with a fist.

Theron's scowl deepened, and with a final shove of force, he stepped clear of his father's chest. As his weight left, the king sucked in a ragged gasp of air, but Theron did not prolong his relief. He stepped back only to widen his stance, then he brought down his scepter with all his strength to the center of his father's chest. The golden crest hit like a hammer.

Bone cracked again, but this time there was no scream. The savage blow winded the king, but his face stretched, his mouth open with agony. Theron sucked in a short breath through his nose and delivered another full-arced blow to the king's already crushed chest. Then another. The audible break was satisfying. The feeling of it rippling up his arm was even more so.

The king's head had fallen back, and there was very little movement in his body. His eyes could not focus and rolled in his head. The blind astonishment in them was mingled with the unmistakable haze of pain. His breath was weak and ragged. Incomplete. It whistled deep in his chest like it was escaping from him no matter how he tried to hold it.

There was blood on the king's broken chest. Not much—just enough to blot the fine white of his nightgown. The color was darker than the wine that stained his sleeves.

Theron felt his own blood boiling in his veins. He itched to eclipse every bit of white with red, cut the king's throat and spill the crimson down his front. Instead, he breathed deeply to settle his pounding heart. He stood still and stared down at the trembling weakness of the creature in front of him.

Ambros' eyes roved through the room, aimless until they found the figure of his son standing there above him, the bloodied scepter still clutched at his side. Their gazes locked, and Theron tilted his head in study.

Rage. Unforgiveness. Hatred. Betrayal. All these things burned inside his father's eyes, and one by one, each of them was snuffed out like a dying candle. Small, struggling sounds escaped the king's lips as he attempted to speak, but only thin, wheezing breaths left him. His venom was spent. His strength was broken. At the last, it was terror that cloaked his father's gaze.

The king's breathing became no more than a shallow pant, and Ambros could no longer look at his killer. His chest struggled and hitched, but it rose less and less with every attempt at air. His moans became weak, his trembling small, and the hue of his skin looked wrong in the hearth's light. Theron watched in perfect stillness as his father's legs gave their last kick for life. The king's chest fell still. The whistle of air lasted for seconds longer after he ceased to struggle.

The room returned to the same silence in which Theron had found it. The fire hissed in low tones as it cast its shadows, but there was nothing more. Pools of red wine spread on the tabletop and on the floor below, their surfaces trembling with reflections of gold. Theron disturbed them when he cast his father's scepter aside. The rod clattered on the stone before it rolled to a stop beside the head of its former owner.

Two emblems of gold lay side by side. The scepter's crest, and the circlet that still crowned its master's brow. Theron desired neither. He left them where they were, their meanings as hollow as the corpse they decorated, and turned to leave the room without another look down.

The door had stayed open behind him when he entered. He passed through the threshold with a tall, even stride and did not spare a glance for the guards who still stood at their post just outside. In the corner of his eyes, he saw how the weak guard still shook, clinging to his spear. But as Theron passed, the man's armor clattered as he struck a full and unrestrained salute.

"My king," he said, his voice ringing clear, but it cracked audibly. Theron heard the man's soft weeping as he left him behind.

"My king." The next guards waited in the room beyond, facing him. Where they had only muttered before, they now spoke with resolution. Their spears were pointed high with respect.

Theron moved between them and forced his way out of the final doors.

The same four men waited for him in the corridor. Four spears locked in perfect salute, and four voices rang out in perfect unison.

"My king."

Footsteps echoed in the stone hall as Theron left these men behind also. The approaching feet were not his own, but he had no reason to question who their owner might be. She appeared only moments later, rounding the dimly lit corner just ahead of him. The witch, Rivia. She stood like a dagger of pure shadow, raven hair glossy in the dark, the smooth skin of her shoulders and arms exposed. The bottom of her skirt was rimmed with blood. She smiled as he approached her, dipping her head in a low, gracious bow.

"My king."

This time, the voice he heard did not echo on the stone walls around him. It was smooth and clear, held only in the most intimate space within his mind. Her silent words were ever like a coaxing caress, tugging at his soul. His heart stirred in his chest.

She said nothing more. There was no reason to. Her very presence had only one meaning, and he accepted it with the slightest incline of his head. Her part in this night's butchery was complete, and her brother would just be finishing with the last. The king lay dead, and his last allies with him. There would be more cleansing to come, surely, but the scales had shifted their balance. This night was over, and the path to the throne was finally opened.

He put out his arm, and she accepted his invitation in stride. Her fingers were stained with red when she wrapped them around his muscle. His own fingers curled into a rippling fist.

He sensed her smile through the dark. "Tonight is the night of your glory," she said, this time with her own voice. Theron's skin prickled. Anticipation crawled beneath it.

He thought of glory and of the dead king in the stone vaults behind him. He felt the movement of Rivia's body in each of her steps, knew her breath in the dimness beside him. A faint smile pulled at the corner of his lips, and their two pairs of footsteps faded into echoes down the corridors of stone.

There would be glory to spare tonight. His reign would begin at dawn.

Caveat Emptor

Marshall J. Moore

"Alright," I said, leaning back in my chair. "Let's see what you've got for me."

Darek reached into the bulging sack at his feet, looking like some greasy parody of the Yulefather as he deposited his ill-gotten wares onto my office desk.

"A canopic jar," he announced proudly, placing a ceramic urn in front of me. "Fresh from the tombs of Nautesh. It has traveled many hundreds of leagues from those dusty sands to you, my friend."

"By way of the duke's own vaults, if I'm not mistaken," I said, dryly amused.

"Perhaps," the portly thief admitted, grinning beneath his waxen mustache. "Though let me tell you, the duke's vaults are a much tougher nut to crack than some pharaoh's dusty tomb, yes? To access the inner chambers—"

I raised a hand, silencing him. "I don't need the details."

"Ah," he nodded, his gaze tracking to the wooden placard pinned to the wall behind me. Words were etched onto it in great block capitals. "Yes. The store rules."

The words etched onto the wooden placard in great block capitals read thus:

HONEST OSWALD'S EMPORIUM
FIRST RULE: NO QUESTIONS ASKED
SECOND RULE: NO LIVE MERCHANDISE
THIRD RULE: ALL TRANSACTIONS FINAL
FOURTH RULE: LET THE BUYER BEWARE

"The less I know, the better," I reminded Darek. "If Sheriff Bryce stops by and asks why I happen to have a Khenatem-dynasty canopic jar in my shop, I won't have to tell him the details. Understood?"

The smile disappeared from beneath Darek's mustache. He nodded tersely.

"Now," I said, reaching into my desk drawer and pulling out a pair of spectacles, "Let's see what you've brought me."

I examined the jar, turning it over in my gloved hands. Like most Nauteshi burial jars, it was capped with a ceramic animal head. This one was topped with a blue scarab beetle carved from topaz.

"It's not cursed," Darek said, giving me a smile that was probably meant to be reassuring.

"I know it isn't." Any curses laid on the jar would have been triggered by its original theft from its distant tomb. "This piece is better than three thousand years old. I'd rather not break it."

I carefully unsealed the lid, and was surprised to hear a faint, rhythmic clicking sound: *klik-klik-klik.* I peered inside and saw a cluster of small black shapes clinging to the wall of the jar, each the size of a grape. One by one, segmented legs began to emerge from them.

I slammed the lid back onto the jar, fumbling in my desk for something to reseal it with. I found a bolt of cotton and wrapped it tight around the lid. Darek watched all of this with a look of mild amusement. "Let me guess. It actually is cursed?"

"I wish it were," I said, collapsing back into my chair. I kept my eyes fixed on the jar. "It's brimming with rustlings."

Darek's face was blank. "Rustlings?"

"Little magical bugs," I said. "Some sorcerer—way, way back—went to the trouble of breeding them from your common garden beetle. Gods only know why. They eat metal."

"Bullshit." Darek stood, his thick hands flat against the table as he loomed over me. He was a big man built of equal parts fat and muscle. I'm built like a scarecrow: all knocking joints and stick-thin limbs. Darek outweighed me by a good five stone.

"You're screwing with me," he scowled. "Trying to drive the price down. 'Honest Oz,' my ass."

I unwound the cloth I had sealed the jar with and cracked open the lid. One of the rustlings slipped out, its soft *klik-klik-klik* filling my office. It skittered cockroach-quick across my desk straight to my letter opener, latched onto the steel blade, and began gnawing away. Within half a minute there was nothing left of the opener but the wooden hilt.

The rustling started to scurry away. I slammed a glass jar on top of it. It buzzed and scuttled angrily, wings fluttering as it searched for a way out.

"I'll be damned," Darek whispered.

I nodded grimly and leaned back in my chair. "I can offer you ten drachmae for the lot."

Darek's eyes bulged. "Ten? Do you have any idea the trouble I went to—"

I held up my hand. "First rule."

"The heist alone cost me damn near three times that—"

"Which was your mistake," I said, my tone polite but firm. "You had the whole of the duke's vaults open to you, and you picked the least-fencible item in his collection: a literal plague.

Honestly, I'm doing you a favor by taking it off your hands."

Darek's slumped wearily into my guest chair. "I can't go any lower than fifteen, Oz."

I restrained myself from smiling. We were in the phase of true barter now. That meant I had him. "I can give you twelve drachmae for the lot. The duke's gonna figure out something's missing from his collection sooner rather than later. When he does, neither of us want Lorrisport's most infamous burglar caught holding the goods."

The praise seemed to mollify Darek. "Thirteen?"

"Done."

* * *

Any city big enough is going to have a criminal underworld. You know the sort: cutthroats and thieves, leg-breakers and bosses, dealers and whores.

Me? I'm none of those. Not anymore, anyway. I'm a fence. I buy things people have acquired through questionable means at a steep markdown, then sell them to whoever's got the coin to pay market value. It's not honest work, but it is work.

The door had hardly closed behind Darek when I heard the bell jingle again. I was busy counting coins—still five drachmae short of what I needed for the month, and with only a day left before rent was due. At the sound of a potential customer, I hurried from my office to the front of the shop.

"Welcome to Honest Oswald's," I said in the brightly cheerful tone I used to set new customers at ease. "I'm Oswald, but you can call me Oz—"

The words died on my lips as I saw who was leaning against my shop counter.

"Hullo, Oz," Sheriff Bryce smiled.

He was a lean man of middle years with a face like a chipped knife. A scar twisted one corner of his mouth up into a perpetual leer, and his icicle blue eyes were alight with cruel humor.

His surcoat bore the arms of the Duke of Lorrisport:

crossed axes in white on a sable field. The same emblem was worn by the pair of watchmen he'd brought with him: a towering set of twins with a reputation for casual brutality. Their names were Graf and Grof, though I'd never learned the trick of telling one from the other.

All three were soaking wet; the freezing downpour that assaulted Lorrisport each winter hadn't relented in weeks. I winced as they tracked rainwater puddles through my shop.

"Gentlemen," I said, recovering myself even as I cursed silently. It was midmorning on the last day of Firstfrost. I should have had an entire day to conjure up another five drachmae before Bryce and his cronies made their appearance. "What can I do for you?"

"Afraid this ain't a social call, lad." Bryce picked up one of the curios on display—a crystal ball formerly owned by a local hedge witch—and examined it, searching its murky depths. "I hate to be the bearer of bad news, Oz, but your rent's going up."

It was a good thing my hands were clasped behind my back, or Bryce might have seen them curl into fists. "Rent" was the polite term he had settled on for "protection money." If I didn't have the drachmae to pay his extortion by the start of each month, I could expect a flaming bottle through my window.

"Why?" I asked.

The sheriff's blue eyes glimmered. "Do I need a reason?"

"I would appreciate one," I said, my nails digging into my palms. "Please."

Bryce's laugh was as cold and cruel as his gaze.

"Fine," he said, "since you asked so nicely. Let's just say that the powers that be have set certain wheels in motion. And for those wheels to turn, they need an influx of capital. Said capital has to come from somewhere, understand?"

"I suppose," I said, moving slowly toward my office. I had left my door hanging open, and the canopic jar Darek had stolen from the duke—the very man Bryce reported to when he wasn't busy shaking down local businesses—was sitting on my desk in plain sight.

"You aren't thinking about reneging on our arrangement, are you?" Bryce asked, tossing the crystal ball in the air and catching it as it came down.

"Of course not." I didn't take my eyes off the sphere, even as my hand found my doorknob. The crystal ball was one of the few genuinely magical items in my possession, and consequently one of the only items of genuine worth. I had yet to find a buyer, but it was only a matter of time before some wizard came to town.

"Good," Bryce said, tossing the ball from one hand to the other. "Because I'd hate for anything to happen to your establishment. It'd break my heart—it would."

Behind Bryce, his thugs snickered.

"I'm sure none of us want that," I said. "How much is this going to cost me?"

"Forty drachmae."

"Forty?" I practically yelped, my cool demeanor slipping.

Bryce's smile widened. "Forty per month."

"That's nearly twice what I'm already paying you, you slippery—"

Bryce hurled the crystal ball to the floor.

I dove for it. Too slow. The delicate globe shattered into a million shards the moment it hit the stone floor, a little wisp of ether rising from it like smoke.

"Forty drachmae," Bryce repeated, grinning. His teeth were sharp and yellow. "I'll be by for it at sundown."

I swallowed. "How am I supposed to—"

"You're a smart fellow," he shrugged. "Figure something out."

He turned to leave, then paused. "Oh, and if you try to skip town or come up short?" His gaze flickered to my office door. "I'm sure the duke will be quite interested in discovering the whereabouts of certain artifacts missing from his collection."

The bell jangled as the door swung shut behind him. I knelt there on the floor, glass shards sticking into my hands like splinters.

* * *

By late afternoon, I was still eighteen drachmae short. I raced up and down the aisles, trying to identify what might be worth enough to use as collateral. So far, all I had was a set of jewelry that had allegedly belonged to the prince of some distant land, a wizard's spellbook three centuries out of date, and a rusting bronze sword that supposedly had some sort of prophecy attached to it.

As I worked, I wondered. Bryce had all but outright stated that the reason for the sudden hike in protection costs was due to one of the lords of the underworld moving against one of the others.

There were three main players in Lorrisport's criminal circles. The Butcher Street Boys were a gang of rough-and-tumble wererats who claimed the poorest, dirtiest quarters of the city for their own. Red Mary was the leader of a clan of vampires and their mortal attendants; they controlled most of the shipping and overland trade in and out of the city. And the Church of Silent Knives was a cult of assassins, who sold their services in the name of a sinister death god.

Right in the middle sat Sheriff Bryce, the duke's executioner. He played both sides of the law and profited regardless of who came out on top. Was it possible that he was making a push to oust one of the factions so he could take over? He was ambitious, that was certain.

I was so engrossed in speculation that I hadn't realized the door had opened until I saw a small, pale man standing at the counter, his eyes darting around the store. He had a large chest behind him, iron-bound and fitted with no fewer than three heavy locks.

"Can I help you?"

He started. His mouth twitched under a prominent hair lip.

"Oh," he said, wiping at his sodden brow. It must have still been raining. "Oh, oh yes. You're Mr. Oswald?"

"Call me Oz. You buying or selling?"

He licked his lips, "Selling."

"I figured." I looked down at the trunk. "Unfortunately, I can't take any more inventory right now. If you—"

"No," he interrupted, eyes widening. "No, you don't understand. I need you to take this."

That put me immediately on my guard. People were only this desperate to fence something when it was a hot item— recently stolen and actively being sought. If I took whatever was in the chest off Hairlip's hands, I would certainly find myself in even hotter water than I was already in.

"Unfortunately," I said, my lips tightening in a thin line that wasn't quite a smile. "I really can't accept anything at this time—"

"I'll pay you to take," he said, digging in his pockets. Gold flashed in the lamplight as he spread a handful of coins across the countertop.

My breath caught. Eight, nine, ten drachmae. More than half of what I needed; it would have easily covered this month's protection if Bryce hadn't hiked up the price.

It might be enough to keep him off my back until I could make up the difference.

He looked up expectantly. I swallowed and nodded. "Deal."

* * *

He left without another word, and I immediately set about trying to open the chest.

My appraiser's eye told me it was an antique, though in excellent condition. Sturdily crafted of rich mahogany, the iron bands holding it together were unblemished. Its three ornate locks differed in their metals: iron, bronze, and silver.

The chest might have sold for a drachma or two if I could find the right buyer. I would need to either dispose of the mysterious contents or squirrel it away until it was safe to move.

Thankfully, I kept a set of bolt cutters for situations just like this one.

I felt a small pang of regret as I cut through the exquisitely crafted locks, but sentimentality was something I had discarded long ago. In my line of work, attachment is a liability.

The locks clattered to the floor, and I heaved open the chest's heavy lid.

Inside was a young woman, curled into a tight ball. Her freckled, doll-like face was in profile, hiding beneath a fringe of blonde hair. Her eyes were closed.

She wasn't breathing.

I acted without thinking—a rarity, I'll admit. I reached in and pulled her from the chest.

She was so small that I could lift her easily.

Her skin was very cold where my arm brushed her cheek, and there was a waxy pallor to her lifeless face.

I sank numbly to my knees and laid her down. A feeling of revulsion creeping through my bones as I realized I was holding a corpse—a corpse someone had paid to dump in my shop.

I didn't recognize her, but that meant little on its own. She could have been anyone.

If the man had been simply trying to dispose of an inconvenient corpse, he could have put stones in her dress pockets and tossed her off a pier—Lorrisport's harbor was a veritable graveyard below the waves.

Stuffing her into a very strong, very expensive chest and dropping her in my shop was a novel approach.

As I was pondering this enigma, I noticed the lamplight gleaming off her elongated fangs.

"Oh, shit," I breathed.

The vampire's eyes flew open. They were wholly black, without iris or sclera. her lips peeled back in a feral hiss. She lunged at me, outstretched hands reaching for my throat. I stumbled back, but she struck viper-quick, landing atop my chest and forcing me onto the ground.

My hands closed around a silver necklace in my pocket.

She hissed again and lowered her mouth to my neck.

I thrust my fist at her—not to punch, but to brandish the necklace.

Supposedly religious symbols work like a charm when it comes to repelling the undead, but as I'm not on speaking terms with any particular deity, I've had to rely on baser measures.

A silver necklace dangled from my clenched fist, reflecting the store's lamplight. I had purloined it early in my career, and hung onto it for good luck ever since—and because—the metal was anathema to the undead.

The petite vampire screeched and flung herself away from me, repelled by the piece of jewelry. It worked like the charm it was. She scurried down the aisle of shelves, pressing herself flat against a rack of secondhand clothes. Her black eyes remained fixed on the silver necklace as I climbed shakily to my feet.

"Easy," I said, holding my other hand palm up in a conciliatory gesture. "Easy, now."

My heart pounded, like it was trying to escape my chest, and it took a conscious effort not to let my outstretched hands shake.

Her shark's eyes flicked up to my face in a quick, calculating glance, then back down to the necklace. There was something deeply disquieting about those inhuman eyes, staring out of her freckled pixie face.

"You're not one of Mary's," she said, her voice reverberating as if in echo of itself. "She doesn't allow any of hers to handle silver."

"I'm not," I said. "And I'm guessing you aren't either?"

She looked away. When she turned back to me her eyes were human and very blue. "Not anymore."

Interesting. For a moment we simply regarded one another warily, her fangs bared, my silver chain held out. Tension hung in the air, and I realized abruptly that she was as scared and confused as I was. Or almost as much as I was.

"Let's make a deal," I said. "You keep the fangs out of sight, I do the same with the silver. Deal?"

She nodded. "Deal."

Moving very slowly to avoid spooking her, I looped the silver chain over my head and tucked it under my shirt, out of sight. "Better?"

She nodded again.

"I'm Oz."

"Alice." She straightened from her half-crouch, glanced over her shoulder at my storefront windows. I had drawn my heavy curtains the moment her container had arrived. It was getting late, but the faintest gleam of sunlight still filtered in between the curtain folds. "How'd I get here?"

I wiped my brow and pointed at her erstwhile abode. "A man dropped you off in that."

Alice frowned. "Pale, nervous fellow?"

"That'd be the one," I nodded.

She sank to the floor, pressing the heel of her palm against her forehead. "Shit, shit, shit, shit."

I'm uncomfortable with emotions even at the best of times, let alone when there's a tiny vampire having an outright meltdown on my floor. I cleared my throat. "Is there, uh… anything I can do?"

She looked back at the curtained windows. "How long until sunset?"

"About half an hour."

She frowned. With her fangs hidden, she didn't look like a vampire at all.

"Can I stay here until then?"

I nodded.

* * *

"I was one of Mary's lieutenants," Alice said. She sat across from me in my windowless office, my thick desk and the canopic jar atop it providing a reassuring space between us.

"Was?"

"She's dead now." Alice looked down at her hands. "Really dead."

A chill crept down my spine. If one of the key players in Lorrisport's underworld was gone, the resulting power struggle to claim her place would see the streets run red.

"How?" was all I could manage.

"They came for us in the middle of the day," Alice said. Her tone was distant, utterly devoid of inflection. "The Butcher Street Boys and their cronies. Someone sold us out. Told them where we sleep through the day." She swallowed. "And they found us. Every one of us."

There was no need to elaborate. The Butcher Street Boys would have made short, brutal work of Red Mary's compromised vampires.

"So, how'd you escape?"

Alice smiled wryly. "I'm small enough to fit in that trunk, and low enough in the pecking order that Braham—my thrall—was able to catch wind of what was happening before they reached me."

I tried not to look discomfited at her casual mention of her thrall—a human bound to the vampire's will. "Braham. The nervous old man?"

"That's him," Alice nodded sympathetically. "He was a…new hire, I suppose. Our bond wasn't strong, and he wasn't smart or brave. He managed to get me away from the Boys, but instead of freeing me he must have dumped me here and run off."

"Don't be too hard on him," I said. "Sheriff Bryce has eyes on all the gates in and out of…"

I trailed off mid-sentence. Bryce. He had warned that wheels were in motion in the underworld.

Which meant he knew about the slaughter of Red Mary's gang.

Which meant he must have been in on it. If anyone was connected enough to ferret out the locations of her peoples' safehouses, it was him.

And he had told me he would be by tonight to collect his rent.

"We have to get you out of here," I said. "Now."

Alice frowned. "It's not sunset yet—"

"It's close enough," I said, rising to my feet. "We'll put you back in the chest until dark—"

She followed me to the front of the store. The chest lay open on the floor beside the counter.

The jingling of my doorbell filled the shop. Before we could retreat to the office, the sheriff stepped into view.

"Well," Bryce said, grinning as the door closed behind him. His icy eyes darted from the open chest to Alice. "Seems you've broken one of your rules, Oz. No live merchandise, isn't it?"

"Technically, she's undead," I said and stepped out of the vampire's way.

Hissing, Alice charged him, her eyes once again glossy black.

Bryce thrust out his left hand. Lamplight glimmered off his silver badge of office, driving Alice backward as though she'd been struck with a physical blow. I stepped forward, putting myself between her and the lawman.

"Seems you've come up with the rent after all, Oz," Bryce said, advancing toward us. He carried iron-tipped mace.

"I don't follow," I said, and began backing away, toward my office.

Bryce nodded at the diminutive vampire. "Butcher Street's put a price on her head worth more'n your shop, lad. Hand her over, and we'll call you square through to next month."

I'd be lying if I said I wasn't tempted. A month without paying Bryce's extortion was a significant space of breathing room. I could stay in business, keep my head low and continue to turn a profit. I'd be safe.

Besides, I was unarmed, and the presence of silver neutralized Alice's vampiric powers. If things came to blows, my odds of getting out alive were slim. Safer to hand her over.

Alice looked up at me, furrowing her brow. In that moment, she didn't look like a vampire. She just looked like a kid, scared and alone.

"No deal," I told him, stepping back and bumping my shoulder against my office door frame.

Bryce's twisted grin only widened. "That's alright, Oz. It's more fun this way."

He lurched at me, swinging his mace. Thrusting Alice behind me, I dodged aside and stumbled into my office, falling heavily against my desk. The canopic jar wobbled violently. I grabbed the scarab-headed jar and turned just as Bryce's mace fell upon the jar, shattering it into a thousand pieces.

Klik-klik-klik.

A dark cloud of rustlings swarmed Bryce's mace. He swung again, but the rustlings had already devoured the weapon's iron head, leaving him holding nothing more than a short wooden rod.

The rustlings overran my office, devouring everything metal they encountered: my inkwell, my bronze curtain rods, even the silver necklace beneath my shirt.

Bryce stared incredulously at the remains of his mace, then at his other hand. Rustlings crawled over his fingers, and his silver badge disappeared beneath their mandibles.

He looked up at me, then at Alice crouching. He stumbled backward like a lost child.

Alice bared her fangs in a malefic grin. She stalked forward, her eyes black and hungry. Bryce cowered against the wall. He caught my gaze, his eyes wide with terror.

"Oswald," he said as the vampire advanced on him, "we can cut a deal—"

"Sorry, sheriff," I shook my head, "rule three: all transactions final."

Bewitching Allures

Avery Davis

"I see an opening ahead..." Rose started, "but it's definitely not any vault. It looks like a cave, maybe?"

Elias squinted, vaguely making out the entrance ahead of them. "I don't have a good feeling about this," he said.

A scoff echoed from Shroud. "And you called Maud and me cowards."

Elias cast a narrowed look over his shoulder at Shroud, then shook his head before pushing passed Rose and stepping into the opening. Maud's torchlight illuminated what seemed to be a vast cavern with walls of jagged and uncut stone.

Elias eyed the bedroll laid out on the ground and the stolen dirty dishes from the castle piled around the cold remains of a fire. He saw no signs of an inhabitant, but his anxious heart climbed up his throat.

Rose kicked one of the bowls on the ground. "Hey, not sure if you notice, but this certainly ain't the vault of riches I was expecting..."

Shroud cursed. "Unless you count these revolting mushrooms as wealth."

Elias heard Shroud spit something to the ground. He closed his eyes and sighed. "Don't put strange mushrooms in your mouth, Shroud," he said, but he quickly put the foolishness from his mind. This couldn't be a dead-end job. He started pacing, pondering what he might be missing. "There's got to be something here. Maybe the switch is somewhere nearby, and there's another hidden door."

Elias stopped when he felt Rose's hand on his shoulder. "Elias, it would take us weeks to examine every nook and cranny of this cave. Maybe we should just—"

"Leave."

The voice was not one that Elias recognized. A chill went down his spine as he turned to the source of the sound. In the darkness of the cavern, he saw a masked figure stepping from the veil of shadows ahead of them. The mask was sleek with black feathers and had a protruding beak like a crow's. Its wearer stood taller than Elias, and was dressed in long black silk.

Shroud did not need to be told twice to leave. Elias caught a glimpse of his companion turning to run back the way they had come. A curse escaped Elias' breath as he watched Shroud abandon the group. Elias would have laid down his life for any member of this team in a heartbeat, but Shroud evidently did not share in such a sentiment.

The sound of a knife scraped against its sheath. Rose readied herself for a fight, her weapon grasped firmly as she took a step back.

"Are you the witch?" Rose called.

Maud was worryingly silent; when Elias looked to her she only seemed to be gazing at the masked woman.

The masked woman stepped from the shadows, though the light from Maud's torch revealed nothing more about her appearance. That is until something glittered at her hip. A jeweled pendant hung from her belt. Elias gazed at it with fascination, he felt drawn toward it.

"Look," Maud started, "we're only here because we thought there were valuables. Since there doesn't seem to be, we'll just—"

"Valuables? You're thieves, then. Despicable," the witch said. She tilted her head at Maud, then looked down to Rose's knife. Elias' gaze repeatedly drifted between the exit, the witch, and the jewel on the witch's belt. "Tell me, what is it that you three value most?"

Rose brandished her knife, and her voice cracked a little when she said, "Coin, of course."

The witch gazed at Rose, then shook her head. "I think not. You most value life, not just your own, but others' as well."

As the words left the witch's mouth, Elias watched Rose grip her knife with both hands.

The witch continued, "And you, Maud? Tell me, what do you value more than anything else in this world?"

Elias could see the uncertainty in his friend's eyes.

"Freedom," she answered. "How do you know my name?"

Apparently satisfied, the witch turned her attention to Elias and ignored Maud's question. His heart froze, he wanted to run but could not move. Once more, his eyes drifted toward the jewel hanging from the witch's belt as she came closer to him. With something as valuable as that he could afford to feed his entire crew for months.

"You," the witch said, when she was within arm's reach from Elias, "I already know what you most value."

Elias made a quick gesture with his hand to swipe the gem, and then stepped back. "And what would that be?" he asked defensively.

"Your friends, your crew." She hesitated. "Your gang of criminals."

Elias looked to Rose, then Maud. "I guess so," he said. "What is it to you? We're just looters, and seeing as there is no loot here, we'll be leaving you in peace."

The witch's eyes narrowed at him through the slits in her mask. "But you have already taken from me, thief. For this, I shall seize what you hold dearest."

The witch lifted her hand to Elias' forehead faster than he could pull away. The last thing he saw was Rose lunging at the witch and Maud running past him toward the exit. Then, a white flash crossed his vision.

The cold night air touched Elias' face. He gasped as he staggered forward, gazing at the surrounding hills. He felt hopelessly disoriented, but slowly recognized the landscape... the smoke rising beyond the trees in the distance.

He and the others had made camp over that way last night. Maybe the witch had knocked him out, or sent him somewhere else. Maybe Shroud, Rose, and Maud had gotten out of the cavern and were now regrouping at the camp.

Elias began a trek toward the smoke over the hills. Whatever had happened back there, the others must be worried about him. As he walked, though, he suddenly remembered the jewel. Elias checked his pocket as he hurried forward. The shining jewel was still there, safe and sound. The witch hadn't taken it back. Maybe his companions had defeated her.

"Rose?" Elias called out as he continued to approach the camp. "Shroud? Maud?" There was no answer, only the crickets chirping around him.

As he made his way ahead, he finally had a view of the campsite. A fire was lit with his companions around it. Maud was confined to a bedroll, though Shroud and Rose sat by the fire laughing with one another.

"Hey," Elias called out to them as he approached, "you left me all the way back there. Kind of rude, don't you think?"

He frowned when Shroud and Rose both went silent and stared at him. Then he furrowed his brow as he watched Rose slowly draw her knife. Maud began to stir from her sleep.

Elias cleared his throat. "It's fine, though. I—"

He was interrupted by Rose standing and threateningly pointing her knife at Elias. "Who in the hells are you?" she said.

"Very funny," Elias said. "But seriously, what happened back there? It must have turned out alright if you're in the mood to make jokes. I'm not hurt, by the way, thanks for asking. How'd you all get out of the witch's lair, anyway?"

Rose and Shroud exchanged a look with one another, and both shook their heads.

"Look," Shroud said apprehensively, "I can tell you are incredibly confused. But we aren't who you think we are, so I think you had best just turn around."

Elias hesitated. What was Shroud's problem? But he shrugged it off and turned to approach Rose instead. She still looked odd pointing that knife at him, but there was no way she would actually swing it.

"Rose, can you tell the moldy potato to leave the bad jokes to you?" Elias had barely finished speaking when she lunged at him, grabbed his shirt, and pressed her knife to his throat.

"I don't know how you know my name, but my friend here just told you to leave," Rose threatened.

"Rose, seriously. Cut it out. I'm telling you," Elias stammered, "we're friends. I've known you forever. You and Shroud, both. We're a team. We met at that market festival where we both tried to rob the same merchant, remember?"

"Sorry, mate," Shroud said, "I've never seen you before in my life."

Maud still had barely stirred from her sleep. In fact, she had barely moved at all, which was strange for someone normally so restless.

Pressing her knife tighter against Elias' throat, Rose insisted, "Who are you?"

"I'm Elias, your friend."

She shoved him to the dirt, and he grunted, but he did not stand. "I think you need to get lost. If you bother us again, I'll cut your throat," Rose said.

Elias remained on the ground, gazing at his friends. The witch had taken them from him. His closest friends had been taken from him, just for one jewel. Elias reached into his pocket once more to gaze at the shining gem, he wanted to scream and hurl it as far as he could. He was never going to rest until he found a way to undo what the witch had done. Elias had never paid the price for anything, and he didn't intend to start now.

Dirty Secrets

Alex Turner-Cohen

Rusty grinned. The young woman had something special, and he intended to steal it.

He'd been watching her for some time now, flitting in and out of the crowd to keep her in his sights. She must have been around twenty, a few years older than him. But where he skulked, she strode. Where he had matted blond hair, she had luscious brown locks. His cloak was little more than a piece of cloth with holes for the arms. Hers was made of velvet, black and shining.

He'd stolen from many people. The rich he didn't worry about, but he lost sleep after taking from the not-so wealthy. What if that old woman needed her purse to pay for a life-saving tonic or if the merchant's daily profits were crucial to prepare for the coming winter?

Rusty had always had a wild imagination. He'd made up stories about who his parents were, why they'd abandoned him on the steps of an orphanage eighteen winters ago. Some days they were loving farmers, and other times members of nobility, with fine clothes and a meal on the table every night.

Rusty was an orphan in Casselton, the capital city of the Cassel Kingdom. Here, the rule was take or be taken from. He knew which one he had to do to survive.

So he kept stealing.

Rusty continued to watch the girl. She checked on a satchel slung across her shoulder constantly, which she clutched so tightly that her knuckles went white. Something important was in that bag, something he would soon have for himself. And she limped. Ever so slightly.

She was asking to be robbed, and Rusty did not want to disappoint.

He pushed through the crowd with the ease of one who had spent a lifetime running and hiding in this city. Pulling out a knife, he flexed his fingers around the handle in anticipation. He twisted his lice-infested hair nervously. This kind of uneasiness was good. It kept him alert, on edge.

Then in one smooth movement, he cut the strap of the woman's satchel. The bag dropped into his waiting hand.

"Stop, thief!" she cried. More shouts followed as city guards rushed to the woman's aid.

Everything about Rusty was in tatters. Shirt, breeches, cloak. Except his shoes. He always invested in a good pair of boots because he needed them whenever he had to run, which, for a thief, was quite a lot.

Now his boots slapped the cobbled ground and he breathed hard. He soon lost his pursuers in the busy city, ducking in and out of its labyrinthine streets.

Panting heavily, he peeked at his prize. And frowned. He'd been hoping for coins and jewels, riches that would pay for supper tonight and many meals to come. Instead, he found a dagger in a sheath. Pulling it free, he realized it was made entirely of black stone that glowed, emitting a faint green light. Lettering was engraved onto both the sheath and blade. The whole thing was rather odd.

Why does the woman need the dagger? All his musings led to the same conclusion: no respectable woman would own such a thing. She was clearly up to no good, so he felt no remorse about stealing from her. Yet, he felt uneasy at the thought that he might have trifled with someone dangerous.

As a thief, he now considered the most important question. *How much can I get for it?*

Rusty headed to Jye's shop in Forgotten Side, just the place where he could sell the dagger. Forgotten Side was overlooked, as it did not appear on any city maps. It was on the eastern edge of the Moonlight River, which sluggishly carried all the discarded waste and dead things. Absent were the lavish inns and colorful shops of Upper Casselton. Instead, beggars of all sorts—blind, deaf, and smart ones—filled the narrow streets. Jye's shop used to be a church. This holy place had become a hub of illegal activity, with smuggled goods and blood money sitting on pews alongside bibles and candles. Sunlight streamed in through stained-glass windows, falling upon the dagger, making it look like a rainbow shard.

Jye looked unremarkable: average height, generic haircut, forgettable gray eyes. Perhaps that was why he was so successful in the smuggling business—he slipped from people's memories like an eel in a fisherman's hands.

But Rusty would never forget him. He'd known Jye since he was six years old, since the smuggler had helped him escape the orphanage. Jye had broken him out of the workhouse where the children had been reduced to little more than slaves. The smuggler had taught him how to steal as a livelihood instead.

"Rusty, my boy, what have you got for me today?" Jye asked, his voice playful.

When Rusty revealed the dagger, Jye reared back.

"Where did you get this?"

"A black-cloaked woman with a limp," Rusty answered. "So, how much will you give me for it?"

"Get that thing out of here," Jye whispered as if a city guard were in the room, hiding behind the shelves. "This blade's been cursed, boy. In fact, if I took it, I'd be committing treason. You know what they do to traitors? Hung, drawn, and quartered. No thank you."

"Cursed? Treason? Hanging?" Rusty's voice rose higher with each word.

Jye sighed. "It's made of seer stone. Someone's parted with a lot of coin for a warlock to place spells upon the sheath. A single touch of that blade causes the victim to die a slow and painful death. It's said the name of the target is written on the blade."

Rusty looked at the markings on the seer stone. But he was illiterate. "What does it say?"

Jye answered gravely, "Montague Fairchild."

Rusty knew the name, of course. Montague Fairchild was the king of Casselton.

Rusty had met His Majesty a few times. The King of Casselton used to visit the orphanage and give the children gifts. He remembered how Montague had singled him out from the others, patting his head fondly and filling his pockets with roasted chestnuts. Everyone else had been jealous.

"I'll throw this cursed thing in the river!" Rusty declared. He wanted no part in this—in a royal assassination.

"No!" Jye grasped his shoulder. "If this woman has a magic dagger, who knows what other tricks she has up her sleeves? Her magic may very well lead her to you. And do you really want her to catch you without the dagger? There's no telling what she'll do."

So Rusty kept it. *Have I seen the last of the woman?* He clutched the dagger more tightly at the thought.

* * *

Brooklyn Wolf cursed. This was meant to be a clean kill, a perfect kill! And then that damned thief had ruined everything. He'd taken the seer stone dagger.

Well, Brook would get it back. She had to. It was crucial to her plan.

It was said there were as many thieves in Forgotten Side as there were fleas on a mutt. Seemed like a good place to start. She turned east and crossed a rickety bridge, entering the slums of Casselton.

Depraved screams escaped from crumbling buildings, a testament to the unholy deeds occurring within. Resisting the urge to hold a handkerchief to her nose, she dropped a coin into a blind beggar's waiting hands as she hurried by. Her limp worsened. All this walking had reopened the deep cut on her thigh. She cursed the thief again.

Brook pitied these people. She'd been like them once. Abandoned. Hopeless. She'd only broken free with King Montague's help.

Brook had been a slave in the salt mines. She'd spent long days in the dark, dust in her eyes, fingers raw and bloody from picking at the quarry walls. One day, she hit her captor on the head with a rock in a futile escape attempt. She was taken before the king to be judged.

Often she wondered what King Montague saw in her that day. Did he really think her a ruthless killer? Or had he seen something else? Loyalty? Devotion? Drive?

Montague had spared her life, allowing her to be trained as his personal assassin: knives, poison, subterfuge. Soon, she was eradicating threats to the kingdom. Outlaws, treacherous nobles, and corrupt tax collectors all paid the price.

The king had given her a new life. And how would she repay that?

With the seer stone dagger.

But she had no other choice. The alternative didn't bear thinking about. She pushed on.

As Brook passed The Wriggling Fish tavern, she saw a body on the ground and stepped over it. A drunk.

There was a puddle of blood under his head. Nothing unusual in Forgotten Side. From the way he was lying, neck twisted at an unnatural angle, he was obviously dead. She'd killed enough people to know.

Brook rubbed her hands together at the thought. She wiped them so often her skin was peeling from the friction. Whenever she looked at her palms, all she saw was the blood of her victims. So she kept rubbing.

In her darkest moments, she wondered if the king had really been lenient the day he spared her. Or had he condemned her to something far worse than death?

Brook turned her thoughts back to the thief. She knew he would try to sell his prize, so she started with fences—people who dealt in stolen goods.

The third fence she came across was a man named Jye.

"I'm looking for a dagger," she said.

"For a fine lady such as yourself, I have many daggers, if you'd like to see 'em." Jye raised his eyebrows.

"It's a particular one. A black one. Made of seer stone."

A flicker of alarm crossed his features. He recovered quickly, smoothing his face into a mask of indifference, but by then it was too late—she knew she had her man.

A little while later Brook left the old church with all the information she needed.

"Rusty," she said, speaking aloud the name of her next target.

* * *

The stench of fish filled the air in Rusty's cramped hiding place—in a lidded barrel previously occupied by fish. The boat was moored to the dock and swayed with the motion of the Moonlight River. This was the best way out of Casselton that Jye could arrange at short notice.

He heard shouting. Then the barrel tipped over, spilling Rusty onto the deck. She stood over him: her black cloak billowed in the river breeze, and she clutched a knife in each hand.

"I believe you have something of mine," she said, sighing.

"How did you find me?"

"A smuggler by the name of Jye."

"He would never tell!" Of that, he was certain.

"You'd be surprised what people say when they have the right incentive." She twirled her knives meaningfully.

"If you hurt him, I swear I'll…"

She laughed. "I did more than hurt him. And I'll do the same to you if you don't hand over the dagger."

Brook stared into the thief's face and hesitated for a moment. His blond hair, prominent chin, soft blue eyes, looked so familiar.

Rusty lurched to his feet and jumped over the side of the boat, the seer stone dagger still in his pocket. The slimy, algae-filled water seeped into his clothes, eyes, and mouth. He writhed in the river, trying to stay afloat. But he couldn't swim. Precious bubbles escaped from his mouth. The silver spheres taunted him as they rose while he sank.

As his vision dimmed, he felt a firm grip on his collar. Someone was in the water beside him—the woman. The dagger emitted an unnatural light from his pocket and bathed her in a green hue. Her hair moved like seaweed as she cut powerfully through the river.

She dragged him out. He spat out water and gasped for air. He lay on the river bank for some time, panting heavily, his pocket empty.

The assassin hadn't killed him. She'd saved him.

* * *

Brook was in the Great Hall. Servants refilled wine goblets, cleaned spillages, and carried platters of food. The scent of roasted boar drifted into her nostrils. A noblewoman with finely braided hair threw scraps from her plate to a dog at her feet. The seer stone blade was tucked into her long sleeve. She wasn't here on official business and hoped her employer, the king, didn't recognize her till it was too late. But dressed in a blue gown and white wimple as a servant, she was basically invisible, especially to the king.

Montague Fairchild sat at the head of a mahogany table. His Majesty had pulled his golden mane into a ponytail for this evening. A well-trimmed beard hid any wrinkles.

Beside King Montague was King Devlin Vance, the ruler of Harland, a nation from the south. Devlin's crooked nose and scarred face were testament to many battles won. And the immense wolf pelt, its head still intact, making up his cloak, demonstrated his hunting prowess.

Casselton nobles dressed in fine clothes mingled with Harlanders in animal pelts. It was a strange sight; the two kingdoms had been at war for generations. Brook noticed a blank space on the hall's left wall, which used to display a tapestry of Casselton knights slaughtering Harlanders. Tonight, it had been diplomatically removed.

Devlin caught her staring and beckoned her closer. She lowered her head and moved toward him uncertainly.

"Bring me some proper ale, girl," Devlin proclaimed, tossing away his goblet of mulled wine in contempt.

She bowed and backed away with the empty tankard. When she returned, she waited for a lapse in conversation to make her move. She slipped the seer stone dagger out of her sleeve and held it in the palm of her hand.

"Promises are all well and good, but how can I trust you will keep them?" she heard Montague tell the scarred king.

"How else can I show you my willingness for peace?" Devlin said. "I have done all I can. Now it's your turn."

She chose that moment to step between them, raising the dagger, ready to plunge it into her king. Before she could touch Montague with it, she felt someone ram her from behind and tackle her to the ground. The breath was knocked from her and she dropped the blade. She recognized her attacker as King Devlin. He rained blows upon her, calling her a murderer and a traitor. She'd been caught.

Just as she'd planned.

* * *

"Be gone with you, boy. We'll have none of your ilk here," a guard told Rusty.

Rusty hesitated as he faced off the two sentinels at the palace gates. He wanted to warn them about the impending assassination attempt, but his resolve was wavering. He was only a thief. Perhaps he should stay out of royal affairs.

But Rusty wanted the assassin to die a traitor's death. Even if she had saved him from drowning, she'd confirmed his worst fears—Jye was dead. And he remembered the king's kindness to him at the orphanage.

"A girl with dark hair and a limp is going to kill the king," Rusty spoke quickly before he could back out. "She has an enchanted knife. You've been warned."

The guards murmured to one another, no doubt unsure if he should be taken seriously. As he started to walk away, they followed. Rusty hastened his stride until he was running.

The castle bell rang urgently.

"You," a guard called. "The bell only rings like that when there's trouble in the castle. What do you know about it, boy?"

They grabbed him.

* * *

Everything hurt. Brook's ribs were cracked, her eyes swollen. Devlin wore rings on his fingers, which had left many cuts on her face. She ran her hands over them and found a particularly nasty one on her right cheek that would scar.

Brook was in a cell. Hay that smelled of waste lined the floor. There were no windows. Wall sconces cast a flickering light about the dungeons.

The click of a lock turning brought her, shaking, to her feet, as the King of Casselton entered her cell. Montague did not seem regal in the dim lighting; he looked old and tired.

"Brook! After everything I did for you, this is my reward?" Montague shook his head. "I thought you were one of my most loyal subjects."

Brook knew she was. If she told him the truth, about the reasons for her actions, her plan would all be for nothing. She made no reply.

"And a seer stone dagger?" he went on. "I had no idea you wanted me dead so badly. And if it hadn't been for King Devlin, I would be."

Though she ached to speak in her own defense, she knew she couldn't. She remained silent. Shouts came from outside the cell.

"Sire, we found this scum outside the castle," a guard said, manhandling the new prisoner. "He was talking about a female assassin and an enchanted knife. The boy must be involved somehow."

The king hesitated when he laid eyes upon Rusty. "Throw him in the cell with her," Montague commanded.

Now Brook realized why Rusty looked familiar. Scrub him clean and dress him in fine garments, this thief would be spitting image of the king as a young man.

With a flick of his hand, Montague dismissed the guards. He circled the thief, scrutinizing every inch of him. The boy squirmed under his gaze.

"So, it's you. Now it all makes sense," His Majesty said. "This was a power play, wasn't it? Kill me and get my bastard son on the throne."

The boy choked. "What are you talking about?"

"Oh, please, don't pretend you didn't know," Montague went on. "You, Rusty, were my greatest mistake. When your mother died bearing you, I could hardly bring you into the castle."

"I swear, Your Majesty, I had no idea," Rusty said. "I've spent years imagining who my parents were. Never in my wildest dreams did I think one of them was royalty!"

Montague paced. "I expected better," he said. "I presumed honest blood flowed in your veins."

His words stung more than all her physical torment.

The king strode away.

* * *

Rusty's head was reeling. He was... the king's son? This assassin not only took Jye, who had been like a father to him, she had also ruined any chance of him getting to know his true father.

"You deserve a traitor's death, and more, after everything you've done," he spat. "After what you did to Jye, after what you tried to do... to my father." The word felt strange on his tongue.

"Jye's not dead," she said. "He wouldn't give you up. I had to convince him I wouldn't hurt you to get him to talk."

"But you said..."

"I say whatever I'm required to get the results I desire."

"You're still a traitor. You tried to kill the king." Rusty tried to sound angry, but now, he didn't feel the same rage as a moment before. Whenever he imagined his parents, he always assumed they were dead. Why else would they leave their son on the steps of an orphanage, to fend for himself, all alone in the world?

* * *

Brook was exhausted from her beating and had almost drifted off to sleep, when she heard a jingling noise. Opening her eyes, she saw Rusty fitting a key into their cell lock.

"What are you doing?" Brook demanded.

"I swiped it off His Majesty when he leaned in close. Folk always underestimate a master thief," he said, grinning.

Brook forced herself to stand between Rusty and the cell door. *For the king,* she thought.

"You can't escape."

"Why ever not?"

"You'll just have to trust me. I'm trying to save the king's life."

"Could have fooled me."

Rusty made for the door. She didn't want to hurt him. But it might come to that. "I found an assassin, bearing the seer stone dagger with King Montague's name on it. She revealed she'd been hired by someone else, someone she'd never met. They provided her with the dagger and a handsome fee to carry out the deed."

Brook touched the cut on her thigh as she spoke, remembering her struggle with the woman. "So I decided to pose as this assassin to weed out her benefactor," she went on. "It had to be believable. The king had to be truly angry. I needed the seer stone dagger, so whoever paid her would think I was their assassin. Now, I'm just waiting for them to come, either to break me free, or more likely, to silence me forever. Then I'll know their identity and I can expose the true traitor. In order for this to work, we have to stay here and keep up the charade until they show their treacherous face."

Brook exhaled in relief, glad to have shared the burden of this secret. And to have someone know she was loyal to her king. She wasn't sure why, but she cared what this thief thought of her.

"I still don't see how that has anything to do with me," Rusty said. "My best bet is to get out of here."

"If you stay here, we can clear our names. We can save the king. But that can't happen until we find out who's truly responsible." She could see he was torn. His eyes flickered from her to the door. She added, "Only the king knows of my existence. If he's killed, I have no one. Please."

Surprisingly, that seemed to convince him. "Fine, but only because you asked nicely."

They waited several minutes. Brook's vision started to blur.

"You don't look too good," Rusty told her.

Brook touched the cut on her cheek. "Poison," she muttered. "Stupid, why didn't I think of that?" She turned to Rusty. "The traitor must have cut me with a poisoned object. So I would be dead by morning, and not reveal their name." She thought back to her capture. "King Devlin was wearing the ring that gave me this cut. But that doesn't make sense. He stopped me. He stopped the assassination."

She remembered how quickly Devlin was upon her. Almost as if he'd been expecting it.

Then it all became clear. King Devlin of Harland had hired the assassin, with the intention of stopping her attack and thereby winning peace for his people. Devlin had wanted peace for years. Her king would be sure to trust him now.

There had never been a true intention to kill Montague. But where did that leave Brook?

* * *

"Repeat back to me what the plan is," Brook asked him.

"Go in the big hall," Rusty recited. "Find Devlin. Pick his pockets. And pray we find some sign of his treachery there."

"Pray he still has the poison on him," Brook amended. "Otherwise, I won't know what I'm dying from. And then there's no chance of an antidote."

"And no chance of ever redeeming myself in my father's eyes."

They had fled the dungeons. Even in Brook's weakened state, she easily dealt with both jail keepers. Two knives were hidden in her boots. With a flick of her hands, she had hit them with the knife hilts, knocking them out cold.

They'd locked the guards in a cell.

"Why didn't you kill them?" he asked. "Isn't that what assassins do?"

She looked at him strangely. "That would be murder."

"But..."

"I've killed many," she admitted upon seeing his confusion. "But the king himself sanctioned all my kills. So I tell myself that's not murder—it's justice."

Traveling through the castle's secret corridors, they ended up in someone's private chambers. Rusty stared. Skillful tapestries, plush rugs, and perfectly crafted furniture adorned the rooms. When Brook wasn't looking, he pocketed a few items lying around.

"We won't be disturbed here," Brook told him. "These are the king's chambers. No one would dare set foot inside without his permission."

Brook slipped into a side room and returned with a manservant's uniform—a dinner coat with floppy lapels and long coattails.

"Change into this," she said.

She inspected him after he put on the uniform. "You scrub up rather nicely," she admitted. Rusty felt his cheeks warming. "But we'll have to do something about your hair."

Before he could protest, she grabbed a handful of his golden locks and chopped it off with her knife. As he gazed into the king's looking glass, he swallowed his complaint. He had to admit, she was rather good with a knife.

She stared at him for a moment. "You look just like him." Shaking her head, she said: "Good luck. I'll be here, waiting." She eased herself into a chair and visibly paled from the effort.

Rusty entered the Great Hall, trying not to seem conspicuous. It was hard. People wore colorful silks and there seemed to be a never-ending supply of food. More food than he'd seen in a lifetime. He had never beheld such extravagance. Casselton nobles conversed with the Harlanders. If things had gone differently, he might have been among them, he reflected.

The Harland King was easy to spot. King Devlin was the tallest man in the room. And the loudest.

Rusty picked Devlin's pocket easily.

* * *

Brook searched the king's chambers for ink and paper. The poison was doing its job, invading her body, making her unbearably tired. All she wanted was to go to sleep, though she knew if she did, she would never wake up. Instead, she forced herself to write a message to her king. The words made her feel ill.

Rusty burst into the room.

"I've got it!" he declared. He held a vial. Black liquid swirled inside.

Brook took the vial and sniffed it. "Mortlock," she confirmed. She felt relieved. "There's a cure that can reverse all the poison's effects. And I know where."

"So all we have to do is get the cure, explain everything to the king, and the invaders will be driven out." Rusty was excited, already opening the door.

"Rusty, we can't," Brook said. "If we prove we're innocent, then that makes the Harlanders guilty. And do you know what that means?"

"We can live out our lives in this castle?" Rusty finished hopefully.

"It means the kingdom's chance for peace will collapse. Casselton continues to fight against Devlin and his army of Harlanders. Thousands will die. Hundreds of thousands." She'd killed so many. But here, now, she had the chance to save lives. Many more.

"I wrote this letter, which explains how it's all our fault," she said. "We take sole responsibility for our actions."

"I don't care about some stupid war! I'm just a thief, I'm no hero."

Rusty tried to grab the letter. She snatched it away.

"This is my chance to live a better life," Rusty said. "I'll finally have a father and a home. I won't go to bed hungry or have to worry about gangs slitting my throat in the middle of the night."

"The king will never acknowledge us, even if we do prove our innocence," Brook said. "I will forever remain in the shadows. You will never be brought into court life. He'll pay you to stay away." More quietly, she added, "We're the king's dirty secrets."

With a growl of frustration, Rusty made a final grab for the letter and went to throw it into the fire. He hurled it to the floor instead. He knew she was right.

"We'll be remembered as traitors and cowards," he said.

"Yes, we will."

He sighed deeply. "So now what do we do?"

"We run."

"But we have nothing," Rusty said. "Only the clothes on our backs."

"Now that's not entirely true, is it?"

She reached into his pockets and pulled out fistfuls of jewelry, including a giant ruby. Being in the Great Hall was an opportunity he couldn't pass up. He had picked many pockets, not just the Harland King's.

"How did you know?" he asked.

"You're a thief. Isn't that what thieves do?"

They looked at each other, then at the stolen goods.

"I know just the man who can give us a good price," Brook said.

They grinned at each other and fled into the night.

Of Things Not Spoken

Mabel Ginest

It was a stormy night when the stranger walked into the Black Brew. Even by the standards of the motley crew that frequented that establishment, he was an oddity. Tall and slender, with aristocratic hands, he was dressed in a billowy black silk shirt tucked into close-fitting trousers of the same color. Clearly of good birth, the young man looked as if he had been shielded from the world by affectionate parents, and was probably unskilled in wielding the ornate sword hanging from his side. Still, there was an unmistakable air of quiet confidence and danger about the man that assured everyone in the tavern that crossing him would be a very bad idea.

"My name," he said smoothly, "Is Zokar Krauzad. I'm looking for a mercenary, who is strong and doesn't mind getting his hands a little dirty." He smiled, and looked inquiringly around the silent room.

"What kind of a job?" one ruffian asked suspiciously.

Zokar removed his black gloves and fastidiously shook the excess water off. Laying the gloves delicately on a nearby table, the man said, "I am in the…medical field. I need an assistant to help me in my experiments and to gather…certain components for me."

One man grunted. "I ain't gonna be a leech's fetch-and-carry."

"Go find yerself a street urchin, you want that," another man laughed. "We have more profitable works to be doin'."

"The work will not be hard," Zokar assured them with another smile, showing teeth that were slightly too sharp, and altogether too white. "Although I must insist on a man who isn't superstitious about working in graveyards at night. I'm afraid I am a nocturnal creature."

All conversation in the tavern abruptly ceased. A necromancer. The man was a necromancer. Even the most ruthless soldier-of-fortune would hesitate before agreeing to work for such a man. The graveyards of Greenwick were considered sacred; no man of sense would dare enter and disturb the rest of those who slept there, especially not to aid in the diabolical, unholy experiments of a black wizard.

"It shall only be for a short time," Zokar promised silkily. "And I will make it worth your while."

There was another long, heavy silence. Then, from the back of the room, a voice said quietly, "I'll do it." Gunner Onyx stood up, sheathing his dagger. "But my services are not bought cheaply." Gunner was a hard man in his forties, with a leathery, tanned face covered in scars.

"Oh, don't worry," the necromancer purred, looking Gunner over. "You shall be paid in full, whatever amount you name."

Gunner just stared at the man, then nodded briskly. "We have a deal."

* * *

Gunner had to admit it wasn't a bad situation. He was being paid nearly twice his usual commission and, at the necromancer's insistence, stayed at Zokar's luxurious mansion.

Zokar himself was undeniably creepy, as was his pale and silent sister, Yoletta, the only other occupant of the house, who spent most of her time in her room. Yoletta was ill, Zokar had told Gunner briefly.

The work itself was relatively easy. All Gunner had to do was slip into the graveyard—just a brisk thirty-minute walk away, on the edge of Greenwick—dig up a corpse or two, and bring them back.

In all, Gunner had robbed more than a dozen graves over the past month, and had never run into any trouble; he was far too capable for that.

Still, after four weeks of the necromancer and his grisly work, even Gunner's iron nerves were on edge. There was just something entirely too normal about the mystic.

"Gunner," Zokar called from his cellar one afternoon. "Come here, won't you?"

Gunner grimaced—he hated the cellar, where Zokar did most of his work—and reluctantly set aside the sword he had been sharpening. He descended the flight of rickety wooden stairs. Somehow, the sterile cleanliness of the white-washed walls and the dozens of beeswax candles made things worse. It felt wrong, somehow, that the place should be so pristine and well-lit. Gunner would have felt infinitely more comfortable if it was dark, dirty, and lit only by a few flickering candles.

The cellar itself was spacious, large enough for a work-table, two chairs, several large cabinets, and a small bookshelf on which were kept tidily arranged notes and a small library of black magic. On the far wall, there was a large door that was always barred. Gunner didn't know what lay on the other side; he never asked, and Zokar never told him.

"Yes?" Gunner folded his arms, standing solidly with feet slightly apart.

"Ah, there you are." Zokar looked up from the corpse he was preparing. "I need another subject for tonight's experiment. He must be a fresh subject. This one," he gestured at the body on the table, "is two days old. I need a subject who is a few hours dead, at most." Zokar grinned at the mercenary. "Will you arrange that?"

Gunner stared at his employer stonily. "Yes."

"Good. I already have a subject in mind. His name and address are on here," Zokar handed Gunner a small scrap of parchment. "Nobody will miss him for a day or two; he should be safe to use. And Gunner, do try and keep the blood loss to a minimum." The necromancer turned back to the body on the operating table dismissively. "Bring him down here straight-away; I'll want to speak to you when you return, so wait for me if I'm not here."

* * *

After darkness had fallen, Gunner lay in wait for his victim, a man by the name of Leonard Torne. It was the first time that Zokar had named a specific person for his experiments, but Gunner was unphased by the development. As far as he was concerned, a corpse was a corpse. Collecting Leonard was just another task to perform.

Gunner didn't know what happened to the corpses. He never saw them stumbling around the mansion after being re-animated, and he never reburied any of the bodies. They just… disappeared, and Gunner—a taciturn man by nature—never questioned his employer.

It was late when Leonard finally stumbled into the dirty, one-room shack, back from a rowdy party. He didn't bother lighting a candle, but just stumbled drunkenly across the room to his lumpy mattress.

Silently as a cat, Gunner came up behind Leonard, and brought him to the ground.

Leonard struggled to get away, but in his intoxicated condition was no match for the mercenary. Gunner calmly put his hands around Leonard's throat, and, almost before the man realized what was happening, had strangled him.

When Gunner returned, the worktable was clear and prepared for the next experiment, but Zokar was nowhere to be seen, so Gunner waited for the necromancer to return.

After ten minutes, he heard the cellar door open. Yoletta walked down the stairs with slow, halting steps. Gunner had met her only once, briefly, at the beginning of his stay at Zokar's home.

She was beautiful, despite the dark, heavy circles under her luminous brown eyes, and her exceeding thinness. Her black hair was thick, but it lacked luster and shine, and was tinged with white, although she was at least half Gunner's age. She didn't notice him at first. Then, as she stepped off the stairs, her eyes met his, and she hesitated. "I thought my brother was here," she said slowly, in a soft voice. "Are you waiting for him?"

Gunner nodded briefly at her, but did not say anything. Like her brother, there was an unnerving air of strange normality about her. Yoletta transferred her attention to the body on the table, her head tilting to one side.

"He's getting close," she said, a small smile turning up the corners of her thin, bloodless lips. "My brother," she added, glancing at Gunner. "All this…" she waved her hand limpidly, the gesture taking in Leonard's corpse. "It's for me."

Before Gunner could respond to this, Zokar came sweeping down the cellar steps. He swirled off his cape and slung it onto a convenient chair.

"Yoletta," he said, his voice unusually tender. "You shouldn't be down here. Go and rest; you need your strength. I'll be up later."

Yoletta drifted out of the cellar, raising one hand absently in farewell. When she had gone, Zokar turned to Gunner, business-like once again.

"Now then. You have brought the subject. Excellent."

Zokar rubbed his long, pale hands in anticipation. He walked over to Leonard and examined the body. He rolled his silken shirtsleeves up to his elbows. "I won't need you further tonight. I have hopes that tomorrow will be an…important day." A strange, burning light sprang up in the necromancer's icy blue eyes, making them shine with an unholy enthusiasm that bordered on mania. As Gunner took his leave, Zokar took up a small, sharp knife and bent over Leonard's body.

Despite the late hour, the mercenary found himself unable to sleep. He was haunted by the memory of the necromancer's wild eyes, fierce in their triumph. Gunner had worked for his fair share of maniacs, but none had ever made so deep an impression on him as Zokar.

* * *

When he awoke the next day, Gunner was immediately and uncomfortably aware of a heavy sense of foreboding. It was everywhere, as if it had seeped into the very bones of the building.

Outside, the air was heavy and electric. Dark, low-lying clouds with a sickening yellowish cast hung over the sun.

By the end of the day, Gunner was keyed to an intensity he had never before experienced. He was so alert that more than once he had been badly startled by the kitchen cat.

As was his habit, Zokar did not emerge from his quarters until well into the evening. The necromancer seemed in unusually high spirits; evidently, the results of whatever experiments he'd conducted the night before had pleased him.

Gunner ate his supper silently and alone, uneasily fiddling with the hilt of his sword until Zokar called for him.

After checking to be sure that his sword was strapped firmly on his belt, Gunner made his way down into the cellar. He paused at the foot of the stairs taken aback by the sight that greeted him.

Yoletta lay on the worktable. She was dressed in a simple white gown and flower petals had been scattered over her corpse and the table.

Zokar was standing at her head, looking down at his sister's face with something approaching tenderness—an emotion Gunner had never seen the necromancer show before—in his gaze. He glanced up as Gunner stepped forward.

"Ah, Gunner," he looked back at his sister's face, and softly, as if to explain, said, "She passed this morning. The illness in her bones had gnawed her flesh for far too long. But I know what to do now."

Gunner left the necromancer to his unholy work. After a minute, Zokar roused himself from the reverie into which he had sunk.

"I have half your wages here." Zokar handed a small, heavy leather pouch to the mercenary. "I have one last task for you. You'll receive the rest of your money once you've performed it."

Gunner took the pouch, weighed it expertly in his hand, then nodded briskly.

Zokar gestured to the barred iron door. "I need you to dispose of the remaining subjects, but tomorrow. Tonight, I have work to do."

Gunner hesitated, then squeezed the moneybag and nodded.

"Excellent," Zokar said. He walked back to his sister's body and stared at it for a moment. He gently caressed her cheek, and said, "I promised her that I would bring her back in the full bloom of youth and beauty." His voice hardened. "And I will."

Gunner waited a moment, then turned and left the necromancer to his work.

* * *

The mercenary had finally fallen into an uneasy sleep when a ghastly scream rang through the house. Gunner sprang to his feet, fully awake, his heart beating wildly. He had never before heard anything like that scream. A few moments later, the same unearthly sound rang through the house once more, followed by a distant crash and a dull, echoing bang.

Gunner cautiously emerged from his room. The only sound was the crashing of the storm. He advanced through the house, one hand on the hilt of his sword. As he reached the cellar door, it slammed open and Zokar burst out; his clothes were torn, and his face and arms bled from fresh scratches.

Gunner barely jumped out of the way in time before he was distracted by a woman's cries. It was Yoletta. She stood at the foot of the cellar stairs, ashen gray, surrounded by a crowd of moving corpses.

Before he could say anything, there was a flash of lightning, followed by a deafening thunder clap; so loud that Gunner felt the mansion shake.

With his ears still ringing, Gunner watched Yoletta lift her head. "There," she hissed, pointing at the two men.

"Shut the door," Zokar told the mercenary, his face white. "Shut the door!"

Gunner needed no encouragement. He slammed the cellar door shut and leaned against it. The door rattled on its hinges as the creatures on the other side banged against it, trying to break through. Gunner knew the door wouldn't hold for long.

"My sister has been suffering greatly these last few months," Zokar said, almost to himself. "She was in pain, unhappy, ill. I eased her passing." He added with a faint smile, "I cannot raise the living, only the dead."

Gunner stared at him. "You killed her."

"A soft pillow over her face at first light this morning." He fell silent.

Behind him, through the door, Gunner could hear the snarls and grunts of the creatures.

Zokar continued, "Her last memory is of me holding the pillow over her."

Gunner grunted as the creatures pushed the door slightly wider than the last time. With an effort, he shoved it closed again, and said fiercely, "I'm leaving. I suggest you follow."

Gunner noticed an acrid, burning smell. Zokar glared at Gunner. "Fire," he said tersely. "Go find it, and take care of it."

"I'm not staying here," Gunner snarled again.

The cellar door rattled more ominously, and as Gunner pushed past the necromancer, it broke down at last. Zokar threw himself to the side and Gunner dropped to the floor, rolling out of the way of the horde that issued from the cellar.

Above them, the upper rooms creaked and gave way, crashing down. Gunner covered his face as a burst of sparks exploded around him. By the time he struggled to his feet, kicking away a burning beam, Yoletta was advancing toward Zokar, who was backed into a corner.

Five of the raised rushed at Gunner, oblivious to the fire licking at their clothing. Without stopping to think, Gunner bolted. Behind him, he heard a roar as the flames gained ferocity, and Zokar screamed something unintelligible. Gunner burst through the kitchen and flung himself through the servant's door, slamming it shut behind him without looking back.

Gunner continued his reckless flight until he was outside the walls of Greenwick, and standing on a small hill overlooking the town. In the distance, he could see Zokar's house burning fiercely like a beacon in the night despite the pouring rain.

* * *

Zokar's estate had been completely consumed by the fire. In the Black Brew, suppositions were exchanged and theories were offered. Gunner was never seen in Greenwick again, although a retired mercenary matching his description surfaced several counties away. Rumors spread of vengeful ghosts—one, a beautiful woman rising from the charred remains searching for someone.

One day a woman entered the Black Brew. She was hauntingly beautiful with thick black hair tinged with white and luminous brown eyes. With fire in her eyes, she said, "I'm looking for a mercenary."

Liar's Tax

Jordan Service

Ugly Larrie was below, standing in the open to receive our client. Her long, red hair swayed as the sad old sap hobbled toward her with his hat held meekly in his hands.

"Did you get it?" begged the old man in a hushed tone, as though the crowd on the street could possibly hear them.

These clients are all the same. I watched, perched from the top floor while Whisper, our enforcer, was inside the building just across the alley, acting as eyes for our blind tactician, Beady. Both ready in case anything went sideways.

With a disdainful expression, Larrie said, "Your mother's urn. Yes, we procured it."

The old man clapped his hat between his hands, his wrinkles pulling up as he smiled. "Praise be! I can't wait to get her home again. Where is she?" He scanned the otherwise empty area.

Larrie's expression remained unchanged, but she slowly stepped closer to him. "One highly decorative urn," she began, "estimated in value by you, the client, at 600 regals, in pristine shape, as you claimed it was at the time of its theft. The item was found by the business—us—two nights ago. The piece was found in pristine condition and remains that way. Final bill estimated at 100 regals."

The old man narrowed his eyes at Larrie who was still in shadow. "Where is it?"

"However," Larrie continued as she stepped into the light, "upon routine inspection, it was discovered that the piece— while indeed an urn valued at 600 regals—had, in fact, been customized magically and subsequently utilized, as a soul jar."

The old man's dopey expression faded slowly as Ugly Larrie continued the recitation of indictment. "The soul jar has been found to be housing an unknown personage. Regardless, the urn's magic has raised the value. At current estimates, an occupied soul jar is valued at... 100,000 regals? That would make the adjusted cost of procurement 16,666 regals. In addition, by *lying to us*, you incur a liar's tax, raising the final bill to a total of 25,000 regals."

This is where our team was the most tense. A lot depended on the client's reactions. The old man's mouth opened without a sound and he dropped his hands mid gesture, wincing.

"A going rate of 100,000 regals?" he whistled at the quote. "They say you can't put a price on life, but, hey, there you have it."

"I have found that's true for one's own life. Others' can be handled at a much more reasonable number," Larrie noted, otherwise unphased.

The old man sat on a shabby crate and rubbed his scalp as he took in the information. "I'm sorry about the deception," he apologized. "People in... this hobby... get used to obscuring information about it."

"Your admission is appreciated, but unfortunately, we do not currently accept apologies as payment."

The old man hunched slightly lower. He lifted his eyes to Ugly Larrie. He took a deep breath and slowly released it as he pressed his fingertips together and his eyes became black. The alley darkened and the noisy streets muffled.

"'Ugly Larrie,' they call you," he noted with deep, distorted reverb. "Why give that name to such a beautiful young woman? Do you, Ugly Larrie, have any idea what I could do to you? What I'm capable of? Not just magically. My work takes creativity and little morality." The old man tilted his head.

"Ah, you're a mage," Larrie said, motioning to the distorted alley. "Then the jar really is for you. You're not just a middle man."

With nothing from the old man but a small smirk, Larrie's body stiffened and she was still. Her jaw tightly clenched. A glowing blue fog surrounded her, and she was lifted to the tips of her toes.

"Do you know how soul jars are made?" his voice rumbled softly. "It's an odd magic. There are few necromantic spells that need someone alive. Of course, you don't stay that way. Instead, it traps you somewhere in between."

"I'm not interested, honestly," Larrie strained to reply. Her eyes stayed locked on him. I was ready for a signal. I knew Whisper was chomping at the bit to crush this fool's head into the bricks of the alley, but she could talk and she refused to give the signal.

I know Larrie well. Her anger, pain, and hatred only fueled her defiance. The more he tried to manipulate her, the more she found deep within herself to resist.

"Oh, no," she responded in labored sarcasm. "Don't use your magic on me."

The old man showed no signs of relenting. "You think your lives are worth 25,000 regals?" he asked. His jaw clenched and his fingers pressed together until his nails were white. His eyes stayed on hers, unblinking.

Larrie groaned through clenched teeth, but she refused to call for us. "Oh, they're worth much more than that," she replied. "It's our lives. But what's the urn's worth to you?"

The old man didn't move. Larrie continued. "If you hurt or harm me, we destroy the jar. If you hurt or harm any of us, we destroy the jar. If you refuse to pay, we sell the jar to a different client to stem our losses."

The old man stiffened his lower lip. A moment later, he released his fingers and dispelled his magic. The light returned to normal along with his eyes and the commotion of the street returned to the alley. Larrie dropped to her knees. She caught her breath and stood, patting the dirt from her legs. Defeated, the old man leaned against the wall and glared at Larrie.

"Well, obviously, I didn't show up here with 25,000 regals."

Ugly Larrie stepped back to her place. "We give you two days. At which point, we will set the location to meet again. If you do not have the money at that time, we sell the jar. If you attempt to hurt—"

"Yeah, yeah," the old man waved her off. "You break the jar." He surveyed the ground. "That's not even what a tax is."

Larrie raised an eyebrow. "Excuse me?"

"A tax is a payment to the government." The old man explained. "This is more of a fine."

"You owe us," Larrie said flatly, "whatever you want to call it. And failure to pay has consequences."

"Maybe we could make a trade," the old man suggested. "I have several pieces that up-and-coming specialists like yourselves could make great use of. Maybe even worth more than you're asking."

"Your offer is generous, but unfortunately—" He rolled his eyes and huffed. "You only accept cash right now, I got it—I got it. I'll see you in two days, I guess."

The old man, standing straighter than when he arrived, walked back the way he came, his hat gripped tightly in his hand. After a few moments had passed, checking all the entry points, Larrie collapsed onto the nearby crate. Whisper stepped out into the alleyway, and I dropped down from my perch. Beady tapped his way out with his walking stick.

Whisper took Beady's outstretched arm. "You alright, girl?" Beady asked as Whisper led him to our huddle.

Still steadying her breath, Ugly Larrie looked up at us. "Am I alright? Do you know what your soul feels like, Beady?

Because I do. I do because I felt it being torn away from me like he was shredding fabric! I can tell where my soul connects to my body, Beady, because it hurts. We don't deal with mages for a reason! From the second we decided to keep the job, everything has been a gamble. I don't like to gamble, Beady."

Beady handed his walking stick to Whisper and reached out toward Larrie. "Listen to me, you wild woman. You own him. He thinks he's somebody; he's a nobody. It's his own fault, trying to trick us and now you own him."

Larrie glared back, making the effort to control her voice. "You talk a good game, Beady, but you weren't face to face with him. He didn't cramp every muscle in your body down to your toes."

"Lare', it's my plan. If you can't trust me, we call it off and walk away. Can you look in my eyes and say you don't trust me?"

Larrie looked into the shadowed glasses and sighed. She placed her hand on Beady's hand with a small smile sneaking to her face. "Fine, you sweet talker. You're right. We've all walked away from all your schemes before. But you're on the hook if he doesn't bring the money."

"Trust me, I know," he answered in a sympathetic tone, "but so far it's all going exactly as planned."

"Besides, what was the alternative?" I jumped in. "We were already too far into the job before we knew it wasn't just a boring vase dispute between two old people. Once the mystic stuff started, we already had the jar. We couldn't walk away."

Larrie shook her head. "We could have played dumb, Tower. We could have taken our hundred regals and been back in bed, safe and sound. Now, we have to play 'keep away chess' with a necromancer."

Beady adjusted his darkened glass spectacles and handed Whisper an envelope. "We're set and ready, Larrie. Since the appraisal, we've done more prep work than ever before. We're making real money this week."

"Yeah, and I'm ready for my part," I said. I bounced a couple of times on my feet. "'That's not what a tax is.' What an arrogant jerk!"

"Tower—" Whisper tried to interject.

"*Tax* is a much better word."

"Tower—"

"It has the word 'axe' right there in it."

"Tower—"

"Who's scared of a 'fine'? It's literally just the word 'fine.'"

"Tower!" Whisper shouted.

"What!?"

Whisper swept his huge arm out in front of him. "He's gotten pretty far ahead. Tailing him is getting harder by the second."

"Right. Sorry." Finally, it was our turn. We started off in the direction toward the old man. Even before we left the block, the excitement was disappearing and the worry set in. Ugly Larrie had a point. Magic was a big gamble if you could use it, and a sucker's game if you couldn't. And we can't.

When we took this job, it was described as standard smash and grab, the sort we accept to cover our basic living expenses. When I cracked the house that held that stupid, beautiful urn, I felt static everywhere. But back then, the only plan was in and out. Leaving the prize behind wasn't really an option.

I made it back to our place with the urn secured, but it was clear this wouldn't just be another quick and easy payday. We discussed. We talked with a guy who knew a guy. Soon, we were in a room full of herby smoke and crystals and whatever else mystics use to tell fortunes or talk to ghosts, hearing some white-eyed nut tell us we were holding the life essence of a poor fool in this jar.

"Play it safe!" Ugly Larrie urged.

"Kill the old guy!" Whisper said.

But it was Beady, our ever-present tactician, who said he had a plan.

"He broke the agreement," he explained, "we cannot do the same. He lied to us. He triggered the liar's tax. We demand it or else we cannot be taken seriously."

I agreed. We have to show potential clients the risk of crossing us.

It isn't enough to threaten with words. We're criminals; that's threatening enough for most people. For anyone already bold enough to seek us out, then double-cross us, we needed more than words.

We've learned that criminals like us are sought out by criminals. Our goal, then, wasn't to scare him into thinking we're going to beat him up. It was to scare him into thinking we'd destroy him.

Somewhere, in his house, in those rooms, there was something he was afraid good people will find out about. There was something that could yank all those respectable bits away. There was something that could mar his name, get him arrested, or maybe even banished. There was something in there that will ruin his perfect life. Hopefully, that life is worth the quote we gave him.

Regardless of how we got ourselves into this mess, we had work to do that night. The liar's tax drives the price of our estimated cost up to the maximum amount. Usually, that means the client has to go extra lengths to get the cash.

We tracked the old man to the gates of a large mansion on the edge of town. Whisper placed his hands on the bars as he looked across the impressive estate. "You mean to tell me this guy is sweating 25,000?"

"Now, now, Whisper," I admonished as I peered between the bars. "Since when does a show of wealth mean generous?"

Night was at its darkest. There was a single light in the front window of the otherwise dim estate. Whisper and I found decent scouting positions and waited through the night.

The old man remained inside until an hour before sunrise. As we hoped, we heard the door slam and saw him with a wrapped bundle under his arm. Some item he was likely hocking to get the money. In his rush to leave, the gate was left ajar.

I nudged Whisper and motioned to the mansion. The final obstacle was the front door. Hoping for similar luck, I lightly pushed the door, but no, definitely locked. And no visible keyhole, either. I squatted to be level with the knob and pulled out my picks. I slid my fingers gingerly up and down the frame until I found a small catch, hidden to the side. A quick press and a small square panel released near the latch, revealing a keyhole.

This was a bad sign. There wasn't enough time to learn where the old man was going, so we had no idea how long he was going to be out. If every move was a puzzle, Whisper and I could get caught at any time. I worked fast until the latch released and we were inside, locking the door behind us.

With the comfort of a barrier between me and prying eyes, I relaxed just a bit. "Alright, Whisp, what does Beady have to say?"

It was true that there was a lot on the line, but the reality was that this worked like any other job. We stepped inside and Whisper pulled out the envelope Beady had given him and opened the note within, reading aloud.

"Step one, get a name. Sounds easy, I know, but you'll be surprised how little your name is on stuff in your own house."

"Fair enough. First order of business: a name," I announced to Whisper.

We moved through the foyer, moving as few things as we could manage. We targeted correspondences, bills, or anything sent from someone else.

"Got something," Whisper called out with a large stack of papers in his hands. I walked over and sorted through it.

"Ah, here we are. Herman Draimer," I said, finding a tax receipt. "That must be the old man. Does it ring any bells for you?" Whisper shook his head. "Yeah, me neither. Now what?"

"Step two," Whisper began, scanning Beady's note, "where's he doing his thing? Maybe it's at his house, but you can't get big magic stuff at the market. He has to have stuff delivered and I doubt he'd want some dirt devil knocking at his door."

"Wow," I said with great disdain. "Wow. Really."

Whisper laughed. "He means like you, you know."

"Yeah, I got it," I spat. "That was like ten jobs ago, man. You try one idea on your own and you never live it down."

"Oh, you know he only does it 'cause he likes you, Tower."

"*First of all,* dirty jobs door-to-door is genius and efficient—"

"You think this is what he's talking about?" Whisper asked, cutting me off mid-defense.

I took it from him and gave it a quick read. "A bill for rental property?"

"Look at the name."

"Bill Miller," I read. "Well, that's fake."

Whisper nodded deliberately at me. "Now the address…"

"This is near the water in the industrial district. Good work, Whisp. Pocket this and restack the letters. Now what?"

"Step three," the note continued, "Now, Tower, you let Whisper take a break if all this reading is too much—Hey!"

"I think that you just read that out loud may mean he has a point, big guy," I smiled with a satisfied grin.

With a dour expression, Whisper returned to the note. "I have yet to know any rich, old guy who doesn't take a trophy from his achievement. Whatever thing he's doing out there, he's got some little knick-knack he likes to keep around to remind him."

"You heard the man, Whisper. Let's go scavenge." We scoured the room until we were satisfied and moved on. Upstairs there were several empty guest rooms and his bedroom, sadly barren of anything except worthless sentimentalities. We finished the top floor just as the sun's rays shot through the window. Few things make me as uneasy as working a job in daylight. Draimer could show up at any time, and we had very little of that left. The only place left to look was downstairs.

Through the kitchen, we found a stairwell. I try to avoid "one entry, one exit" areas, but I was in a hurry. I was hoping to find everything we needed without having to go down at all.

The smell of basement musk and alcohol sat heavy in the wine cellar.

I wished I had known about wine. I could make a few hundred regals if I just knew which bottles to grab. I shook my head. Wrong time for that. To the back of the room, there was another door.

Whisper pointed. "That's either where he keeps the good stuff, or it's something dangerous. Either way, it's locked."

And what a lock! Obviously custom, it was huge and heavy, shaped like a silver brick with a shackle thick as an adult middle finger. My nerves had only gotten worse. Still, I pulled out my tools and set to work.

My hands started a little shaky, but I'm a professional; it didn't last. So, when my lock picks broke inside the padlock I was shocked… It had to be magic. I would never be that careless.

Panic was really setting in. The sun had risen and we only had a name and an address near the docks. We needed to get into this room. Looking around the wine cellar, I saw the display that held the wine corkscrews and improvised.

"Whisper, grab one of those lever-action openers and come over here. Now, look. This may not work, but I'm going to talk you through this. Alright?"

Whisper dutifully took one off the wall. "Why me?"

"Because my idea is brilliant, but my body is weak. Improvised tools, improvised plans—"

Whisper shook his head and lifted his hand. "Whatever, Tower, just tell me what to do."

Teaching wasn't my strong suit. I turned my entire focus to the lock. "First, take the point of the corkscrew and place it in the block of the padlock, on the top, at the point the shackle connects. Now, press as hard as you can and start levering."

Whisper did his best, grunting all the way. "You know, *ugh*, I'm strong, *mmph*... But I don't think I can just yank the innards out."

"We're not doing that, Whisp. Just separate the shackle from the catch. Hopefully, that's all it takes." Quietly, I dreaded some magical thing that no one could account for. Not all magic is illegal. Surely, if you have enough money, you can put something on a lock and no one would know. So, in thinking about the magic, it never occurred to me that this lock may be mundanely booby-trapped.

With a final grunt from Whisper, the shackle popped and the door opened as a plume of gas erupted in his face. His eyes rolled up, his knees buckled, and he fell flat on his face.

My heart dropped with him. "Whisp? Whisper. Whisper, get up, man."

My job is to pick locks, steal valuables, and sneak out. So far, I'd broken my picks, dropped my partner—a body bigger than I can carry—and taken nothing of value. Right then, I could only *just* manage to keep from crying.

Thousands of options rushed through my head. First, *run*. It's a classic for a reason. We were here on borrowed time as it was, and the old man was due back any second. I could take what I had and get out before there were two bodies lying on this floor. It might be enough.

But Beady carved this plan from marble, down to the personalized notes. Larrie had stared down this necro while he tried to rip her in half. And Whisper wouldn't leave me. To fail here would be a betrayal. If I was going to go forward and live with myself, I couldn't leave him here. Not yet, at least.

I tossed the corkscrew back where it came from, grabbed Whisper's ankles, rolled him to his back, and dragged him into the newly opened room. I hoped this poison was temporary. Door shut, safe inside, I dropped and pressed my fists into my head. The plan was going wrong. Prison would be next. I'd be tortured to give up my friends. Then we would be executed. Unless this old man found us first—

"Shut up," I whispered to myself. "Shut up, Tower. That isn't happening. Back to work. Get back to work."

Dread has to be caught and released before it stops paralyzing. Somehow, Larrie can do it in the midst of conversation. I need *all* my focus to clear my head. With two deep breaths, I lowered my arms, and with a more stable mind, I reached into Whisper's pocket and pulled out the note.

> *Final notes: remember, we think he's a necro-*
> *mancer, so if it fits that look, grab it. Dirt, bones,*
> *blood, whatever. If he has a zombie chained up*
> *down there, we want a chunk of it, you get me?*
> *If it's some other thing, if he's laudering money*
> *or wrote down a plot to kill the king, toss that in,*
> *too, but most importantly, get out and get back.*
> *Whisper can knock stars into people's eyes, but*
> *it's up to Tower to make this whole thing worth*
> *it. You'll both be good. Y'all always are.*
>
> *P.S. Make us rich, guys*
> *-U.L*

Beady's words in Larrie's handwriting grounded me. I took inventory of the area. There was a raised table in the middle of the round room. Shelves held various sized jars filled with dirt, all labeled with a date, place, and a name. The smell, though. Off setting the taxidermy feel, there was an alcohol smell that was too harsh to be coming from the wine outside.

My first impulse was the jars. If I had understood the labels, that might have been a stopping point. From among the many choices, I found a small vial filled with a dark soil that fit neatly in my pocket.

The work area, with locked cabinets and hanging tools arranged by length in neat rows, just screamed, *I'm hiding treasure!* Among the tools were several thin, long wires I could bend into usable picks. I was eyeing a couple of good pieces when I heard the front door above us close.

This was exactly the worst place I could be. Trapped in a cellar, right in the middle of his den of guilty secrets. I tracked the sound of his footsteps. With luck, they would tap up the stairs and stop at his bed. Old men needed sleep, didn't they?

Instead, they moved toward the kitchen.

"Don't panic," I whispered to myself. "Don't panic." *Let's see where this goes.* "Don't panic." *We didn't leave any signs we're here.* "Don't panic." *Maybe he just needs a drink to calm his nerves before bed.* "Don't panic." *Stop saying "Don't Panic" out loud, idiot!*

The steps were louder, hitting the tiled kitchen floor and then heading directly to the wine cellar.

It was time to gamble: Stay still or run. What would he do? Is he the kind of person who would take comfort in checking on his hidden lair, or was he paranoid enough that he wouldn't want to draw any accidental attention to it? *Paranoid* being a relative term here, since he had, in fact, been followed.

Then Whisper started to move.

I froze in my position and slowed my breathing.

The man took a couple of steps, stopped. A couple more, stopped.

He's browsing! I thought with relief. In ten, twenty minutes, *we'll be home free.*

I sprinted to Whisper, his eyes still closed. I covered his mouth with my hand and leaned over him, holding a finger to my lips and a desperate expression on my face, waiting for him to look up. His eyes slowly blinked open as the footfalls ascended to the kitchen.

"He's upstairs," I whispered. "I'm breaking into this cabinet. We'll leave once I'm done. Just be still and quiet for a little while longer."

Wincing, Whisper nodded.

I lifted my hand from his mouth and moved back to my picks and the lock. With a quick shimmy and push, the cabinet popped open. Inside sat an ornate, wooden jewelry box that looked quite out of place amongst the sharp metal tools and cold slab rocks that made up the room. I pulled it out and applied my picks to it.

Inside were rings. Dozens of rings of all different sizes and make. I pulled one out, thinking we had stumbled upon some incredible loot, a treasure of magic rings, now at my disposal! But close examination (and a life of experience) told me otherwise.

I showed one to Whisper. "Know what this is?" I asked, motioning to the design on the top.

Whisper, too tired for a guessing game, only shrugged and pressed it back to me.

"It's why we're here, Whisper. It's a signet ring. A lot of signet rings! Trophies."

I showed him the open box. His newly-awakened eyes blinked heavily as he focused on its contents. Then his eyes rolled up to me. "So we're done here?"

"Yes, Whisper," I said. I took all the rings one-by-one and placed them in various pockets, trying to keep them from touching anything that would make them clink as we made our way out. "As soon as Draimer is asleep from his glass of wine, we'll scoot ourselves right out the door."

We had completed our grab and had nothing but to wait for our escape.

Anxiety has an interesting effect on time. Accurately measuring the half an hour for wine to fully pull a person into a deep sleep is hard. Minutes feel like hours.

In an effort to stay positive, I dreamed of new tools, food both healthy and delicious, and maybe even a splurge on some new clothes. Every sane burglar's goal is getting out of burgling, and we never had a job worth so much. 6,250 regals a participant, if my math was right.

I'd been saving for some time, and while this payday wouldn't quite buy me a house in a new city, I could set myself up for the foreseeable future. By the time I was picking out a humidor in my mind, it was time to gather up and make our move.

I inched the door open. Whisper was finally on his feet and behind me.

"How do you feel, big guy?" I asked as I readied for our escape.

"Half dead," he grumbled. "But I've been getting better. I can walk."

"Considering you should be all dead, I'm happy. If it comes to it, can you fight?" I asked.

"Yeah," he answered as he braced himself on the wall.

No, I corrected, mentally. Despite what he wanted to believe, he was dead weight. Without a bruising option, I focused all the more on the quiet option.

I pushed the door back and managed to get the massive lock to relatch.

Up the stairs and through the kitchen we went, and then into the foyer. There, slumped in his big chair, was old man Draimer. His wine glass was empty and nearly slipping out of his drooping hand as he snored loudly.

On tip-toes, we moved right behind him and out the front door. Turning back, I flipped open the hidden keyhole and locked it again. I pulled Whisper behind me while I ran to the fence and scaled the gate. We nodded to each other and split up.

I sighed in relief as I forced myself to walk at a casual pace. We made it.

The whole team met that night and we moved to the final phase. I handed over the bill, the vial of soil, and the rings to Beady who worked those raw materials into something truly valuable. We pulled out a piece of parchment and Ugly Larrie refined Beady's ideas with eloquence on the page. She wrote out the address on the mortgage bill, copied the information on the vial, rubbing a little of its dirt around the words. Finally, she pressed each ring into ink and stamped each seal under the body of the letter.

We placed the letter with the soul jar while Beady, nearly shaking with excitement, walked us through the rest of the plan.

The following night, we set up in the original place. We sat the urn in the middle of the alley with the note rolled into one of the handles while the rest of us took our places, Whisper behind the door, Beady under the window of the opposite building, and Ugly Larrie and I up top to get a good view of the action.

Right on time, Draimer, bag in hand, walked into the apparently abandoned meeting point. He looked around and made his way to the soul jar. He put his bag down and pulled out the note:

> *Dear Herman Draimer,*
>
> *We regret our absence in this handoff, however we are certain you should find your item in perfect condition. We ask that the money, please, be dropped carefully through the open window to your left. Before you think about leaving without payment, I ask that you consider what the authorities would find at 1366 Waterfront. Or why you would have this cemetery dirt from 1200, Oak Wood, Jessa Primm. They might also find it suspicious. Though, it might seem suspect why you keep a trophy box of signet rings from missing or dead nobles.*
>
> *This is the liar's tax, Mr. Draimer. If you leave without paying, we leak the information. If we find the money is short, we leak the information. If you hoped to dupe us, but are now worried, drop the money you have and walk away with nothing. Otherwise, we hope you enjoy your purchase. Thank you for choosing us for your procurement needs.*
>
> *Regards,*
> *Concerned Tax Collectors*

Draimer read the note, rubbed his finger over the grit, studied the imprint of the signet rings, and took in all the bits we dug out of his house.

There's no reason for us to be bluffing now. Still, I could see hesitation. No one around. Why put up with this? Why not snatch and run?

But Beady's plan was too tight. I kinda wanted to see him try for both. We've never had to truly devastate anyone before. I wanted to see what would happen. In the end, though, what made this a good plan was that Beady knew exactly what Draimer would choose.

"I was never going to cheat you!" Draimer yelled through the alley. "It's all here! I'm sorry it came to this, but it's done now. You have your—'tax.'" With another paranoid glance around, he threw the money bag through the open window, picked up his urn, and walked away.

We waited until we were certain he was gone and met at the base of the building. I already planned my route to the tavern and Ugly Larrie was planning on buying the first round. Whisper was waiting on Beady to walk out with the cash. I stepped ahead of him and opened the door to the money-drop. Under the window laid Beady's walking stick and dark glasses next to a rolled-up paper.

Larrie picked up his glasses as I unfurled the paper, where written were only the words:

Thanks, and sorry.

Larrie was breathing with an effort. Her eyes pooled but she refused to let a tear fall. Her grip on Beady's glasses tightened until the frames bent and the lenses cracked.

"He lied to me," she managed through gritted teeth. "He lied! To me!"

"He's—he's not even blind?" I managed to say as I stared at the writing on the note.

"I don't get it," Whisper said, staring at the stick on the ground, "where'd he go?"

"What's there to get, Whisper?" I snapped, waving the letter at him. "He conned us! He played us, waited until the stakes were huge, then he stole enough money to start a new life somewhere else!"

I kicked Beady's cane across the room as hard as I could. "He's gone, Whisper. He left us nothing. Larrie stared down a necromancer, you sucked down poison gas, and he left us nothing!"

Collective Fantasy

Shards dropped from Larrie's hands and dropped to the ground. She brushed off the remaining bits of glass and smears of blood on her hand, then looked at us. She spoke with a professionally controlled voice I knew well, "There's a tax on lying to us," she said, "and we don't accept apologies."

Games

Anne Gregg

"Come to free me, princess?"

The footsteps alone told Lethe who was there. Lethe waited in the dungeons for nearly a day. The darkness of the cell didn't bother her; sure, the ebony stone walls, with faint hints of dried blood, were stifling, and she had to do her "business" in a bucket but to lay on the floor? That was the worst of it. It was honestly a surprise her "savior" hadn't come sooner. If made to wait another day, she would have been tempted to escape, but she reminded herself a royal pardon would come as it always did.

"How'd you know it was me?" asked a delicate voice.

"Because." Lethe kept her gaze on the cell wall, ignoring the princess as she threw a concealed knife, cleanly slicing off a golden lock from the princess Riona's immaculate head. "I wouldn't be good at my job if I couldn't tell."

"You could have killed me!" the princess stammered.

"You should appreciate the mercy. Besides, I'm not about to kill my new employer now, am I?"

Riona's lavender eyes glittered. "A band of robbers stole enchanted weapons from the royal armory. They were last seen in Fyn District, causing trouble and harming shopkeepers and their families. Two children have already been struck down. I need you to stop them before they hurt anyone else." She handed Lethe a scroll, granting her an official pardon.

"Example or silently?"

"Silently. We're not monsters."

"You may not be, but I am," Lethe said as she watched the princess unlock her cell door.

"You have a heart in there somewhere."

"All monsters have hearts," she whispered in Riona's ear, causing a shiver to run down the princess' spine.

The princess cleared her throat and said, "When you've finished the job, meet me at the place you grew up."

Lethe pretended not to be affected by this choice of rendezvous and waved the scroll in triumph as she disappeared up the stairs that lead to the grand palace. She kept her head high, despite how oppressive the architecture felt: the vaulted hallways tried to challenge her, to make her small against the crowd of nobles, advisors, and guards, all rushing in and out of meetings, some eyeing her suspiciously. The members of the king's entourage recognized her father's visage in her features, only softer. He was the king's top advisor and much admired in his time. That was before his untimely passing.

She pushed past them and out into the dark streets. The moon was gone, and clouds covered the sky, leaving the city a black void.

She detoured to her hidden cache, retrieved her requisite accouterment, and proceeded to the seediest part of town: Fyn district. Just south of the smelting facility, she focused her ethereal ear, which gave her the ability to sense magical use nearby, and waited.

* * *

For the first few hours, she picked up benign magic use, such as healing or lighting a dark space, but eventually, she perceived a flash of malicious energy.

She rushed toward the surge as a male patron attempted to flee the building, but a blue streak of light struck him down.

She unsheathed her shimmering longsword and approached the fallen figure. He lay unconscious and quivering. She felt his pulse; it was hot to the touch.

She walked through the entrance of the Three-Eyed Boar as a drunkard stumbled past her.

"Let him go. He won't get far," said a blond man beside the counter.

The blond, a brunette man, and a bald man surrounded the barkeep. The blond was intimidating the proprietor with a flaming blade. The brunette held a sparking blue bow at his side, which quickened the air with static. Beside him, the bald man stood stiff with two mystical daggers at his hips; they were without form or light, which were by far the most lethal weapons in the room.

She neutralized him first with her impossible blade, imbued with the thinnest edge conceivable. It sliced down his neck and spine. He collapsed to the floor without an utterance.

The brunette glanced at his fallen compatriot; no wound was immediately visible.

"Jax?" he said dumbfounded and turned to Lethe, who was already raising her blade to strike him. He reacted just in time to block the attack with his bow. As it made contact, wisps of lightning showered sparks through the air.

The brunette swung around the bar and fired an arrow. As it released, the arrow disintegrated into lightning. It missed Lethe by inches and streaked across the room, hitting a boar head, setting it ablaze.

She swung again, but once more, he blocked her with a smirk. "Don't you know that elder weapons were forged with ancient metallurgy? They cannot be broken."

"Is that so?" she said, smiling. She stepped close to him and sliced his hand off in one stroke. "It might as well be broken now."

He screamed and fell to the ground, cradling his bleeding stump.

She turned her attention to the blond and the barkeep, who stood frozen, the molten blade still between them.

"You move, and I'll burn him to ash!" the blond screamed.

"You can kill him, but that sin is on your head, not mine."

He frowned and raised the blade toward the barkeep. It glowed molten orange, spitting fire. The barkeep whimpered and braced himself for the blow that never came. The blond pushed him down and faced Lethe. He held his sword in a defensive stance.

"This blade will incinerate yours," he said as he swung down, melting through her blade.

Before she could react, a shriek interrupted their duel. The brunette, who had crawled to retrieve one of the mystic daggers, had mistakenly touched the blade when prying it out of his dead comrade's clutches. The abyssal knife started to absorb his fingers and palm. He haphazardly flung it off his left stump before it could capture more of him. Lethe grabbed it midair and threw it, piercing the burning boar's center eye. The cursed dagger slowly devoured it and then itself.

Lethe grabbed the second dagger and aimed at the blond. "Pick an eye."

He dropped his sword, and the flames vanished. "Look, we're coin-snatchers, not murderers. We just wanted to have some fun before delivering them to their new owner."

"Who would that be?" she asked, raising the dagger to eye level.

"She was cloaked. I didn't get a good look, but she spoke like a high-born and lavender eyes."

Lethe narrowed her eyes and knocked the blond out with the hilt of the dagger. She gathered the magical weapons and departed.

* * *

The princess waited alone by a gaslight underneath the burned husk of a fallen tree.

"Still no escort?" Lethe said as she approached. The site of Lethe's childhood home filled her with memories both joyous and tragic. It was now only an ash heap. She had come home from the market to see it blazing. Her mother, father, and younger brother were all inside when it burned down.

Riona flushed and said, "Escorts have ears and mouths." She smiled at the magical weapons. "Hand the love-lies to me."

"You don't really care about 'murdered' children, do you?" And then added under her breath, "Looks like you're a monster after all."

"Well," Riona scoffed. "You needed to be properly motivated. These fools are not the Knights of the First Order. I knew you would quickly dispatch them and return."

"They were just thieves you hired to steal from your own family," Lethe said, flipping the dagger in the air. "For what vile purpose were these intended? Remember, I never miss."

The princess laughed nervously. "Oh, you're going to give me another haircut? Please, put down the dagger. We need to talk about an assassination, and I would prefer to discuss it civilly."

Lethe shook her head, spinning the dagger's blade in the air slowly. "Oh, Riona, who do you plan to assassinate?"

"I'm not going to assassinate anyone. You're going to assassinate the king."

She stopped spinning the knife and looked up at the princess. "I refuse. I did the job required to secure my royal pardon. Here are your spoils." She dropped the fire blade and the bow before the princess' feet, keeping the dagger.

"Oh, but you will do this job," Riona said with an arched brow.

"And why would I do that?"

"We want the same thing, deep down," she said, giving a coy smile, "You just don't know it yet."

"How so?"

"This is not the first time these weapons were used in a monstrous manner. Do you see that knoll there?"

Lethe nodded, recognizing it as the one she sled down during winters past.

"On that very hill, this bow fired an arrow into the heart of the king's top advisor. A man who was too popular to execute, yet who could not be allowed to live, for he dared to speak against the king's injustice."

Lethe wasn't sure if she believed it possible.

"And a pair of abyssal daggers had been plunged into the backs of his beloved wife and son. No witnesses could be spared."

Lethe's heart sank. "I cannot trust your words, princess."

"And this sword, it set the lovely estate ablaze."

"I..."

"Do you not trust me still?"

"Do you trust me?" Lethe retorted.

Riona walked up to Lethe and ran her fingers down Lethe's arm. Riona brushed her hand as Lethe tried to sputter out, "Still, how can I work for someone who—"

The princess leaned close and placed a gentle kiss on Lethe's parched lips. "Tell me, do these lips lie?"

Lethe stood motionless.

"Come, my pretty monster, we have preparations to make."

Lethe obeyed and gathered the elder weapons. Then she stepped out of the fallen shadows of her former home and into a new era.

Author Bios

Elizabeth Suggs

Elizabeth Suggs is co-owner of the indie publisher Collective Tales Publishing, owner of Editing Mee, and is the author of a growing number of published stories, two of which were in a podcast and poetry journal. She is the president of two writing groups, one being part of the LUW. She's a book reviewer (EditingMee.com) and popular bookstagramer and cosplayer (@ElizabethSuggsAuthor). When she's not writing or reading, she's playing video/board games or making cookies.

Jonathan Reddoch

Jonathan Reddoch is co-owner of Collective Tales Publishing. He is a father, writer, editor, and publisher. He writes sci-fi, fantasy, romance, and especially horror. He has been working on his enormous sci-fi novel for over a decade and would like to finish it in this lifetime if possible. Find him on Instagram: @Allusions_of_Grandeur_

Alex Child
Writing has a unique power, and Alex Child is just smart enough to know that he's nowhere near smart enough to accurately describe it. Between working half as hard as he should and twice as hard as required at his day job, he continues pursuing that indescribable emotional swell from relating to a literary character and sharing their experiences. He hopes his story brings you even just a portion of that rush.

H.R.R Gorman
H.R.R. Gorman fashions dark stories by night and makes drugs by day as a pharmaceutical process engineer. He grew up in the Blue Ridge mountains of North Carolina and was the first person in his family to attend and graduate college. He obtained his bachelor's, master's, and PhD in chemical engineering and now has come back to North Carolina with his nuclear engineer husband and vicious attack-Pomeranian. In between processing pharmaceuticals and delving into fiction, Dr. Gorman likes playing Dungeons and Dragons. You can find more of his writing in the *Dark Divinations* and *Lethal Impact* anthologies, at www.hrrgorman.wordpress.com, or on Twitter @hrrgorman.

W. J. Lewis
W. J. Lewis is an actor and writer based in London. He recently co-created and co-wrote Itv2/Hulu tv series *Zomboat!* As a writer/performer he owned Radio 4 series, *Strap In It's Clever Peter*, with his award-winning sketch group. He has most recently performed at the Edinburgh Fringe Festival and toured Brazil with his one-man comedy Western show, *GUN*, which received many favorable reviews and which he is currently transforming into an

audio project. Whilst he is working on his debut fantasy novel, this is his first published short story.

E.G. Thompson
E.G. Thompson writes under several names and has published short stories and books in the fantasy, science fiction, romance, and satire genres. Some of her shorter works can be found in magazines such as Broadswords and Blasters, MYTHIC Magazine, and SQ Mag, and Flame Tree Publishing's Heroic Fantasy and Bodies in the Library anthologies. She works as a librarian during the day.

Jesse Chen
Jesse is a walking Asian-American stereotype trying his darndest to shoulder two generations of immigrant expectations. You've heard this story before: piano lessons, math competitions, teacher's pet—tack on an insecurity complex and nonexistent social skills, and you've almost got the full picture. He graduated from Harvard and sold his soul to a bank in New York, but everything changed when he began writing in the fall of 2019. It began with crafting stories on Reddit. It grew into contest entries and finally led to penning a full manuscript. The rush of developing a story, honing the prose, and sharing that emotion—it was something else. His heart became set on a new dream; to write life-changing books for kids.

Zoë Freeman
Zoë Freeman is a writer based out of Pleasant Grove, Utah. She works professionally as a marketing copywriter and copy editor, but her passion has always been for fiction and fantasy. Her interest in wordsmithing took root at a young age and she attempted her first novels at ages nine and ten—tales of pirate capture and dragons. Her skills have since matured, but she keeps those manuscripts as a reminder of her original dreams. Zoë loves character-driv-

en stories that explore relationships and the complexities of human hearts. She uses her writing to support herself, her husband, and their cat, Tuna.

Allison Tebo
Allison Tebo is a Christian writer committed to creating magical stories full of larger-than-life characters, a dash of grit, and plenty of laughs. She is the author of the *Tales of Ambia*, a series of romantic comedy retellings of popular fairy tales and her flash fiction and short stories have been published in Splickety, Spark, Inklings Press, Rogue Blades Entertainment, and Pole To Pole Publishing. When not creating art with words or paint, she enjoys reading, baking, and defending her championship title of Gif Master. You can find out more about Allison on her website, www.allisonteboauthor.com or via Facebook.

Avery Davis
Avery Davis is an author who was born, raised, and grew up in the city of Bountiful. She still lives there today, with her two dogs and a whole lot of cats. In her free time, she loves to travel to interesting places and has a longstanding love for Swiss chocolate. She writes most days and her first book, A Thief's Lies, is a medieval dark fantasy book containing both intrigue and action. You can contact Avery Davis and follow her on Twitter: @AvaDavisWriter and Tumblr: @FaeFoolery

Marshall J. Moore
Marshall J. Moore is a writer, filmmaker, and martial artist born and raised on Kwajalein, a tiny Pacific island. He has traveled to nearly thirty countries, sold a thousand dollars' worth of teapots to Jackie Chan, and was once tracked down by a bounty hunter for owing $300 in overdue fees to the Los Angeles Public Library. He lives in Atlanta, Georgia, with his wife Megan and their two cats.

Mabel Ginest

Writing has always been an important part of Mabel's life, and she knew at a very young age that she wanted to be an author. One of her earliest attempts at creating the next bestseller was at seven years old when she wrote an amalgamation of Shakespeare's *A Midsummer Night's Dream* and the Greek myth of the Minotaur. Since that time, she has greatly enjoyed using her fertile imagination to craft innumerable stories, all with a quirky, fantastical bent to them—she still hopes to hit the bestseller list someday, but as long as she can write she's happy. During the summer months, Mabel works in a local greenhouse and has amassed quite a bit of information about a variety plants… which she often uses to her advantage in her writing. She currently lives on her family's farm with her cat, Polly, and far more books than she has bookshelves.

Alex Turner-Cohen

Alex Turner-Cohen is a 21-year-old creative writing student and journalist from Sydney, Australia. She's currently working on a fantasy novel with her twin sister involving dragons. Alex can spoil any party by going on a long rant about everything that was wrong with the ending of Game of Thrones.

Jordan Service

Jordan Service a husband, father, and amateur writer. Many people say of him "He talks too much about music, math, and philosophy," to which he replies "Wanna hear about a fractal symphony I just learned about? I'm pretty sure it's beautiful."

Anne Gregg

Anne Gregg is a 17-year-old writer and poet from Northwest Indiana. She started writing when she was in elementary school and hasn't stopped since. Currently, she is her high school creative writing club's 3-time editor-in-chief.

Right now, she's working on a series of political fantasy novels and a Dungeons and Dragons musical (although it's not going well). But, as an increasingly nihilistic person, she has decided to put her work out in the world sooner rather than later.

Want more?

Check out future anthologies at
www.CTPFiction.com